The Devil Tree

Books by Jerzy Kosinski

Novels

The Painted Bird
Steps
Being There
The Devil Tree

Essays

Notes of the Author
The Art of the Self

Nonfiction
(*Under the pen name Joseph Novak*)

The Future Is Ours, Comrade
No Third Path

The Devil Tree

by

Jerzy Kosinski

New York

Harcourt Brace Jovanovich, Inc.

First edition
ISBN 0-15-125328-5
Library of Congress Catalog Card Number: 72-88804
Printed in the United States of America
B C D E

To Katherina
and to the memory of my mother

Author's Note

This book is wholly fiction. Any resemblance to the objective present or past is gratuitous, and similarity to any actual event or character is accidental and not intended.

Sometimes the future dwells in us without our knowing it and when we think we are lying our words foretell an imminent reality.
—Marcel Proust, *Remembrance of Things Past*

The native calls the baobab "the devil tree" because he claims that the devil, getting tangled in its branches, punished the tree by reversing it. To the native, the roots are branches now, and the branches are roots. To ensure that there would be no more baobabs, the devil destroyed all the young ones. That's why, the native says, there are only full-grown baobab trees left.

He leaned against the steel balustrade at the end of the street, looking down at the East River. On the sidewalk behind him people sunned themselves or walked their dogs. Across the river, jets were taking off in rapid succession; their silver bodies shimmered for a moment in the bright sun, then disappeared, leaving behind only a thin line of grey exhaust which disintegrated before the next plane's ascent. On the near side of the river, a helicopter hovered over the water, casting its shadow on a red-and-blue tugboat, then shot off towards the city skyline. Another helicopter descended and touched down, quivering to a stop on the landing pad.

He walked towards the heliport, where three freshly painted blue-and-white copters sat on the platform. A large sign proclaimed: "SEE MANHATTAN FROM THE AIR. A DOLLAR A MINUTE. EXECUTIVE HELIWAYS, INC." He went into the ticket office. "I would like to take a trip around Manhattan," he said to the clerk behind the counter. The man looked him up and down without smiling.

"A trip around Manhattan? Why don't you take a subway, and save yourself the money?"

"You can't see Manhattan from underground."

"Then take the bus."

"How much is a half-hour flight?"

The clerk leaned towards him across the counter. "Look, son, I got no time for jokers. This is Executive Heliways, not bum-ways. Understand?"

"I'm serious." He reached into his pocket and pulled out two crisp one-hundred-dollar bills. "Will this do it? I want a half hour of flying time."

The clerk stared at the money. "I'll check with the pilot." He disappeared into the back room, returning a moment later with a man in a grey uniform. "This is the fella who wants to take the ride," he said.

"Look, son," the pilot began.

"I'm not your son. I'm Jonathan Whalen, and I had a father of my own. Here's the money." He pushed the two bills towards the clerk. "Now let's get started."

The pilot and the clerk glanced at each other. "Mr. Whalen," said the pilot, "I'm going to have to—" he hesitated—"sort of frisk you before take-off."

"You frisk everyone who flies with you?"

"Well, no. It's what you'd call, at our discretion."

"It's up to the pilot," the clerk interrupted. "He's the boss. No frisk, no fly."

"All right," said Whalen. "Go ahead."

"It's easier if you put your hands up," said the pilot. Whalen obeyed. The man's hands rapidly patted his shirt and leather pants. "Take off your boots," he directed, and Whalen obeyed. The pilot peered into both boots, then returned them. "Let's board," he said.

They walked to one of the helicopters and climbed in.

The pilot turned to Whalen. "Now, listen," he said. "We're gonna do the metropolitan area, see all the sights, and come right back here. No tricks. Start acting funny, and I'll dump you out over the Statue of Liberty. Get it?" He pulled the throttle. The machine coughed, vibrated slightly, then arched off the ground. They flew towards midtown, cruised over Central Park, and along Fifth Avenue. Binoculars flashed from a terrace on the RCA Building.

"Every time I fly in a helicopter," Whalen said, "it reminds me of the model gyros I had when I was a kid. It's like being guided by remote control."

"Yeah," said the pilot. "Well, now I'll show you where they keep all the money."

The helicopter turned south towards the Battery. As they approached Wall Street, Whalen pointed to the old-fashioned skyscraper to the right of the Stock Exchange. "Could you fly over that one for a second?" he asked. "I've never looked down on it. I always saw the tops of other buildings from it. My father used to tell me their names."

The pilot glanced quizzically at Whalen, but said nothing as he guided the helicopter over the harbor, circled

5

the Statue of Liberty, and then headed towards the Narrows, trailing the wake of a large ocean liner.

"Okay," he announced. "End of the line. No trip to Cuba this time, my friend."

"Why Cuba?"

"Let's just say you sorta look the part."

When they returned, Whalen noticed a police car waiting next to the landing apron. The helicopter hovered over it for a moment, then touched down. Whalen stepped out immediately, ignoring the spinning rotor over his head. Two policemen got out of the squad car and approached him.

"That's the guy," shouted the clerk.

"Put up your hands, fella. We wanna see what you got on you," ordered one of the policemen. He shoved Whalen against the helicopter door and started to frisk him. He removed Whalen's wallet from his hip pocket and opened it. "Jesus," he muttered to his partner, "this guy's carrying over two grand." He turned back to Whalen. "Where'd the money come from?"

"A bank," Whalen answered. "The one we just flew over."

The policemen stared at the clerk. "What the hell's he talking about?"

"The money," answered Whalen. "I cashed a check today."

"Where do you live?"

"Nowhere yet. I just got here. All my things are at the air terminal."

The policeman reddened. "Listen," he said. "Either you tell me what I want to know or you'll be sleeping in jail tonight. How come you don't have any identification?"

"Why should I?" said Whalen. "There's no law in this country that says I have to carry identification papers."

"Listen, kid, don't give me any crap about your rights. Where's your family?"

"My parents are dead."

"Okay, I'll give you one more chance. Either you tell me where this money came from or we book you for vagrancy."

Whalen shrugged his shoulders. "It's a beautiful day. Why do we have to go through all this? Call Mr. Burleigh at my bank. He'll tell you where the money comes from. National Midland. Mr. George Burleigh."

Whalen and the two policemen walked over to the office. One of the men stayed at the door with him while the other went inside to make the call. He returned a few minutes later and handed Whalen the wallet. "Mr. Whalen," he said, "I'm really sorry about this." He laughed nervously. "You know, there are a lot of creeps —that is, uh, a lot of strange-looking people—walking around these days and when Heliways called us we had to check you out. A routine precaution, you know. I

7

realize you're really a fine young person, but you look—"
He searched for a word but couldn't find it. "You know,
you never can tell." He paused again. "Can we give you
a lift somewhere?"

"No thanks," said Whalen. "There's no place I want
to go right now." He turned and walked past the office,
where the pilot lounged in a metal chair pushed against
the wall, drinking a cup of coffee. Whalen stopped. "How
many helicopters are there in the air over New York right
now?" he asked.

"I guess about twenty-five."

"And how many people are they carrying altogether?"

"Maybe sixty."

"Sixty people looking down at twelve million," said
Whalen. "That's really something. For thirty dollars you
can spend half an hour looking down on twelve million
people."

"Yeah," said the pilot. He leaned forward. "Say, if you
don't mind me asking, what does a guy like you do for a
living? I mean, not everybody carries around that kind
of money. What's the secret?"

"There's this money in a bank," Whalen answered. "I
live on the interest."

"You live on the interest? That's nice. What happens
to the money?"

"It becomes mine when I reach a certain age."

"No kidding," said the pilot. "And when's that?"

"Next week," answered Whalen.

It was night and he was surrounded by people of his own kind who spoke his lánguage and lived in his city. His audience was the young people embracing on the sidewalks in front of bars or leaning against motorcycles and double-parked cars. Yet they were alien. He had already dismissed them. He was his own event.

A girl walked towards him, her raincoat open to show off her tanned legs. Whalen looked into her face as she passed, but she didn't return the look. He considered following her. Perhaps, perhaps he should. Perhaps.

He walked into a restaurant and made his way through the packed tables to the bar. Mirrors reflected the light from a pressed-glass chandelier, shooting glittering prisms into even the darkest corners of the room.

I've bought the smallest tape recorder available. It's made to look exactly like a pack of American cigarettes and it records everything from a two-minute memo to a four-hour conversation on very thin wire which doesn't need to be reversed. It operates on its own rechargeable battery and contains an invisible condenser microphone which self-adjusts for voice distances even in a large conference room. I keep it in my pocket and can activate or stop it at any time, merely by pressing it with my thumb.

Look, man, I'm just being friendly, that's all. I was standing behind you in the line at the bank. I saw you writing something on that little piece of paper, right? You gave it to the cashier and then he handed you all those travelers checks. Not even a check. Man, you have some sonofabitch of a contact in this bank. That's doing it better than the tellers do it.

You know what they've got going on the side, don't you? They take down the name and address of every old lady and widower and faggy loner and other rich bastard who comes in with a fat little savings or check book. Then they sell the creep's name to certain guys in this town who want to know where those kind of rich numbers live. Some of these guys pay up to a hundred bills for one good name. A hundred bucks for a lousy address!

Of course, these guys know how to make their bread pay off. They visit a bitch in the middle of the night and rip off her jewelry, or maybe they convince some poor lonely queer that he should try sharing his stash if he wants to enjoy living a little longer.

And how about those dudes in the removing business? They have a nice thing going too, huh? It's good to know you can avoid a big hassle when you split from a sticky out-of-town broad. All you do is call a number and they give you an appointment at a certain address. You pretend to your chick you're going to look at a new apartment and you want her to go along. The minute the two of you show up, some guys and their chicks appear. First, they push you around so your broad will think you really tried to save her. Then, they lay a hundred bucks on you for delivering her and throw you out.

Now for a few days things will be rough on her—particularly if she's tightassed about not spreading wide for guys she hasn't been introduced to or if she doesn't dig sucking lesbies she didn't go to Sunday school with. But after a week or so, she'll learn how much true love goes for in Fun City, and it won't seem so bad. And anyway, what do you care?

Listen, Whalen—isn't that the name you wrote down for that teller?—what I'm saying is that you and I can really score in this town.

Man, it's so simple. You get yourself a partner—like myself, say—and then you go to the bank and buy maybe two thousand dollars' worth of travelers checks. You sign your name on the top, like the bank says, but you do it so your friend can copy the signature. Now when you split the bank, you cash some of the checks yourself —let's say five hundred and fifty bucks—then the next day you go back to the bank and say you lost the rest of them. The bank has to give you a set of replacements. In a couple of days you come back in and cash them. Meanwhile, your partner's been busy at some big hotels or another bank, cashing his own set of checks.

You know, a smart guy can do a couple of thousand dollars' worth of checks in a day or two—he can double your money. Of course you have to be careful. The banks don't dig getting shit kicked in their faces, and people have been doing this number a while now. You'd need an I.D. and the other guy would have to be straight-looking, with a shirt and tie, shoes, the whole number. Then you could really start raking off the bread. Dig it?

I find it hard to decide if the psyche is a source of energy or of impotence. As I become more and more aware of myself, I see myself divided. My most private, real self is violently antisocial—like a lunatic chained in a basement, grunting and pounding the floor while the rest of his family, the respectable ones, sit upstairs, ignoring the tumult. I don't know what to do about the family lunatic: destroy him, keep him locked in the cellar or set him free?

Since I left home I have been a vagrant, an outcast; that has been my justification for living in the present and refusing to examine my psyche or my past. But if I am to know myself, I will have to confront my contradictions and admit the impact of my childhood. Karen said that she envied other people their pasts. She did not say she envied mine.

When you were born, Jonathan James Whalen, the moon was moving into the last quarter of its cycle. This moon phase indicates that you will experience crises in your thoughts more often than in your actions. You suffer from a lack of flexibility where principles are involved. Sometimes you force issues. It is hard for you, Jonathan, to take criticism. You pretend to see humor in situations that are not really funny. Other people's evaluations of you are a challenge: you react by claiming to take yourself lightly.

Your fixed sign is Saturn. Saturn indicates feelings of separation and estrangement. Having to leave familiar surroundings may well be a part of your destiny. Saturn also makes you hard on yourself. You are too impulsive, and have difficulty sticking to things. You must acquire patience and stability. You must protect your mental, physical and financial resources. You have great gifts: do not squander them.

On the crossroads outside Bangkok I used to wait for the villagers driving their carts home from the market.

The drivers, who smoked opium all day, trusted their donkeys to find their way home, so that by the time the carts reached the place where I waited, the men were asleep. I would leap out of the bushes, approach each patiently trotting donkey and turn him around. The cart drivers never wakened. One day I turned twenty carts around.

It's fine stuff, I tell you, fine stuff. When you smoke it, you know you can't give it up but you make that decision each time you reach for the pipe. When you don't smoke, you feel abandoned. It can't grow too far from the sea, hates snow, favors certain winds. On some days it shrinks, on others it swells. It's best with dim light, soft carpets, large beds. But it's deceitful. You never know when it will turn against you. You don't need other people. What for? Sure you can imagine them around you but you don't have to put up with their actually being there. Even when you don't increase the amount, the effects change. The stuff does weird things to a man: contracts his pupils, suppresses his sex drive, but increases his heartbeat. It slows down a woman's blood but speeds up her desires. You smoke it yourself, lay it on your woman, and will she make love! Meanwhile, you lie still, your eyes shut, your mouth dry. You're at the mercy of a strange love that sucks all your juices. With every smoke you see waterfalls turn into ice, ice into stone and stone into sound. Sound turns into color, and color becomes white, and white becomes water.

I met Barbara in Rangoon. She introduced me to several American and British expatriates, among them a Mrs. Llewellyn, who had stayed on there after her husband died. One day she invited Barbara and me for lunch at her house, which stood on a hill sheltered by tall trees, overlooking the Gulf of Martaban. She lived alone. Once a week a Burmese servant and his helper came to clean the house, the large garden and the swimming pool.

During lunch, Barbara complained to Mrs. Llewellyn about the hotel we lived in. The old lady suggested that Barbara and I stay in her house while she went off to visit a friend for two or three days. Barbara and I gladly accepted.

I helped Mrs. Llewellyn ready her car for the trip and she left the following day. The house was peaceful. From the terrace we watched the ships moving towards the port and the yachts crisscrossing the bay. A liner entering the harbor was immediately surrounded by small rowboats.

In bed Barbara said, "It would be nice to have a house of our own just like this one. We could stay in it, smoke our pipes and not be bothered by anyone."

"I can get rid of Mrs. Llewellyn, if you want," I said.

"What do you mean?"

I shrugged. "Oh, I don't know. She's alone in the world. No one would notice if she didn't show up, would they?"

Barbara laughed. "Don't be silly; this isn't Hollywood. Go to sleep. Sweet dreams."

Later that night I tried to wake her to make love, but she didn't respond.

The day the old lady was expected back, we waited up past midnight. When she hadn't arrived by one, we decided to go to bed. An hour later we were awakened by the sound of her car. I got up, and told Barbara to go back to sleep, that I would help Mrs. Llewellyn unpack.

When Barbara woke me up in the morning, she was already dressed. "Where is Mrs. Llewellyn?" she asked.

"What are you talking about?" I said.

"We heard her arriving last night, and you said you

17

were going down to help her with the car. She's not in her room, and her car isn't here."

"I don't know what you're talking about," I interrupted. "I think you must have dreamed it. Nothing like that happened last night."

She became angry. "Stop playing games. Where is Mrs. Llewellyn?"

"I suppose she must be somewhere. Everybody is. But if I were you, Barbara," I insisted, "I wouldn't bother about it any more."

Barbara stormed out of the house, slamming the front door behind her. Through the window I watched her examining the soft sand of the driveway for traces of the car. She came back up to the room, visibly upset. "What did you do to her, Jonathan?" she asked. "Where is she?"

"Stop it, Barbara. You know very well that there's nothing I can say. Let's go swimming and enjoy ourselves." Barbara put her hands on my shoulders and looked up at me.

"What have you done with her?" she asked again.

I pulled her towards me and kissed the inside of her ear. "Please, Barbara, I told you: forget it." She pushed me gently towards the bed.

"Please tell me. What have you done with her? Was it—was it quick? What if they find the body?"

"This isn't Hollywood, Barbara."

"If I'd known you meant it, I never would have—"

"Let's go swimming," I said.

As we sat by the pool, I could sense her restlessness. Twice she went back to the house to investigate the driveway and the adjoining park. Each time she returned to the pool she looked at me as if she were seeing me for the first time. I pointed to the cabana and told her I wanted to make love there. She followed me inside without a word, but as we were screwing she asked me what I had done with Mrs. Llewellyn's car. I said nothing.

Once she realized that we would not be interrupted, Barbara felt more secure in the house. She began smoking as much as I. She would move towards me and caress my body and ask me if I had made Mrs. Llewellyn suffer before I killed her.

One morning she recalled a story I had told her before we met Mrs. Llewellyn: I was in a bordello on the outskirts of the city. The madam noticed me looking at a ravaged old woman and offered her to me. When I objected, the madam said that for a hundred dollars I could do anything I wished to her. If I wanted, I could kill her, "with that," she said, pointing to my loins. The madam explained that the old woman had been a prostitute all her life, that she was almost eighty years old now and would soon die. She had no relatives; if I agreed, at least her funeral would be paid for. When Barbara asked if I had killed the woman, I said nothing.

During the night when Barbara was still aroused and

I was spent, she provoked me into beating her. In the morning she showed me her bruises and insisted that, to make up for the pain I had caused her, I should tell her what I had done to Mrs. Llewellyn.

For the next two weeks we smoked several pipes every day. Towards the end I got sick. My heart fluttered often and my pulse slowed. My forehead, palms and feet became cold and sweaty. Diarrhea kept me pinned to the toilet and I vomited constantly.

Once, when I stumbled exhausted into the bedroom, I found Barbara lying in Mrs. Llewellyn's large bed, smoking and listening to the radio. She looked at me coldly and said that, unless I told her what I had done to Mrs. Llewellyn, she would not help me. She would let me die. I refused. She lay there, calmly watching as involuntary shivers seized my body. I collapsed beside her and lay trembling until sleep finally came.

The next morning we heard a car pulling into the driveway. Sluggishly Barbara got up from bed and dragged herself to the window. Suddenly she screamed and ran downstairs. Mrs. Llewellyn was struggling to get her large suitcase through the front door. When Barbara returned to the bedroom she tried to control her voice. "Why didn't you tell me?"

"Tell you what?" I said. "That I gave the old bag money for a vacation in England?"

At first I was afraid that I would be left defenseless, that I would babble aloud the things I've always been terrified of saying. Instead, opium made me realize that I could say anything I liked without losing my identity.

But the inner peace I sought was not to be had so easily. Opium simply proved that my feelings were complex and changeable. My awareness increased, but I found no answers. Every word, every gesture became significant and multilayered, defying interpretation as mere speech or mere act.

"I am high," I said to myself. "I know I am high, and I want to use my state to free myself. There are things I want to say and do that I wouldn't dare otherwise." But I never did them. My predilection for self-repression, not liberation, was heightened. It seems that what I really want is a drug that will increase my consciousness of others, not of myself.

Barbara's dress and slip fell onto the floor. She awkwardly grasped her panties and drew them down to her knees. Her face was very flushed and wet with tears.

Moistness blanketed her body. Her touch left my skin cold and damp. When we kissed, her tongue seemed swollen and too wet. It was as though I were kissing the moist blind mouth of a five-year-old.

The next day Barbara and I moved to a small hotel. A few days later, while I was still sick, she left me.

When I returned to Rangoon after my cure, I found her in a hospital, receding under the grey sheet that was drawn tight across her shoulders, separating her head from her body.

She told me she wanted to be committed, to lie in a bed and be put to sleep. She loved the idea of death, of taking a needle and plunging it into her heart or of jumping from a skyscraper.

Her face was puffed and her body shrunken; her thin neck seemed unable to support her head. Her eyelids closed slowly, as if they were sticking painfully to her eyeballs.

Karen called from out of town. She sounded disturbed. She said she realized that I was right: there was a dependence between us that went beyond mere physical intimacy.

I remember a letter she sent me once. "With you," she wrote, "I feel the reverse of that fear I usually feel with others. I'm sure you'll accept the parts of me which are complex but I'm not so sure about the parts that are ridiculously simple."

I told her I had always wanted to conceal both portions of my own personality: the manipulative, malevolent adult who deceives and destroys; and the child who craves acceptance and love. Now I know that I have really tried to conceal the child at the expense of the adult. My dominant concern has been with not admitting needs, not asking for things, not squandering money.

My worst terror has always been that I will seem helpless, that appearing childish I will again be judged in relation to my parents.

The spring before I left, I lay on the football field, pulling up blades of grass, piling them up beside me, a book open in front of me. The wind scattered maple pods onto the pages, rippled through my jacket, and blew my hair across my face. Karen sat next to me. She announced that she was going to visit her mother for a few weeks.

The days before she left were depressing. Every evening we drove around for hours, and one night at the top of a long hill we ran out of gas. I remember climbing down to the circle of lights in the valley, and climbing back up in a cold wind, with a can of gasoline in one hand and a peppermint-stick ice-cream cone in the other.

One afternoon as I strolled barefoot around the lake I saw her standing in the doorway, her hair tumbled about, her skin tanned, with her pink-and-white-striped blouse half unbuttoned. She walked to her car and drove away, while I continued along, feeling physically dislocated, wishing I could dissolve into sun and wind.

"Next year is important to me," she had said. "It's a chance to have fun and to grow up. It's a good college, and besides, there's not much I can do here. I want to enjoy life, maybe even model. Be free to dash off to Paris, to go to Morocco for Christmas, to ski in Austria and Switzerland. To meet German, French, Italian men. To sip warm beer in Dublin pubs, and invite friends for dinner at my apartment in Rome. Now I have the chance and it won't come again. I don't want to waste time being miserable over an adolescent love affair."

I remember how, as a boy, I used to collect the cork tips of my father's cigarettes and stick them in my stamp albums. I believed they contained his unspoken words, which one day would explain everything.

I have not changed. Now I explore my memories, trying to discover the substructure hidden beneath my past actions, searching for the link to connect them all.

"Your mother was very anxious to keep you abroad, Jonathan. In fact, she was desperate." The doctor avoided facing Whalen. "In her nightmares you appeared buried as the unknown soldier from Vietnam. She didn't want you to be drafted. As long as technically she didn't know your whereabouts and couldn't forward your draft documents only you remained legally liable. Still, your mother was very disturbed about not knowing where you were."

"I was on the move."

"Well, yes, that's why she was upset. She imagined you with long hair and a beard, wearing Army fatigues, hitchhiking through Burma, India or Africa with a knapsack on your back and a beat-up guitar slung over your shoulder. We never knew where you stayed." He scratched his neck. "That time you were ill, it took the Burns people four months to locate you. Until then we had always known approximately where you were through your habit of writing your checks on scraps of paper and giving them to the closest bank to clear funds in New York. As I recall, you wrote your last check in Ankara for thirty thousand dollars, or was it thirty-five? Before that you'd lived for several months on less than one-third of your allowance. In any case it exceeded your trust allowance of twenty-five thousand a month but the trustees unhappily allowed the check to clear. Then, your abandoned Jeep was found but you had disappeared. You could have been anywhere. You might have been dead. Your mother was frantic. She had no choice. Acting on my advice, she hired detectives to locate you."

"How did they find me?" asked Whalen.

"They traced you to a group of American hippies in

Katmandu. Finally they located you in one of the prisons in Calcutta, or was it Bangkok? Apparently, you had desecrated a temple; you either entered it naked or you undressed inside. They managed to have you released and delivered to the doors of the American Embassy. At the time, you were very sick. Your withdrawal must have been very painful. You may not even remember it all."

The doctor put out his cigarette. "During that period your mother was hospitalized several times. To avoid unnecessary publicity her nurse would call us whenever there was danger of an attack and I would personally bring her here to the hospital. Your mother often refused to co-operate, even though it was obvious that for her own sake she should be put under treatment. Sometimes we had to—" he paused, searching for the words —"tranquilize her. Actually, though, she loved it here. Once she arrived, she never wanted to leave New Haven. That's how my staff and I know so much about you, Jonathan. The bank and the trustees called me continually. And your mother spoke about you often. She always kept your photograph on her night table."

"What photograph?"

"You as a child standing next to your father."

"How did my mother die?"

"Since your father's death your mother had been a very sick woman."

"Did she kill herself?"

27

The doctor paused for a moment. "It was an accident, really," he continued. "She kept all her medicine in a small refrigerator in her bedroom. Somehow, perhaps when the refrigerator was being defrosted, the bottles got so wet that their labels slid off. That night your mother took medicine from the wrong bottle. That's all. A tragic accident."

"Was there an autopsy?"

"No. Why? She was under my care."

"Why would she keep such strong drugs in her bedroom?"

"When your father died, all the stresses and demands in her life suddenly stopped. It was a tremendous letdown. Suddenly her life had no purpose."

"I was still alive," said Whalen.

"Well, yes. But you had failed in school and had taken drugs, you had gotten into trouble with that girl—"

"Karen—" Whalen broke in.

"Yes, Karen. It was decided you might be better off living abroad. So your mother, perhaps the first time in her life, was completely alone."

I remember a luncheon given by the parents of one of Karen's roommates. We had all been invited down from school. After lunch, the parents went to their country club to play cards and golf, the other students went swimming, and I was left alone with Karen, who stood at the door watching the cars drive away. I pushed her hair back from her face and kissed her neck. Her face colored, but she stood still and said nothing. I slid my hands under her blouse and cupped her breasts. She closed her eyes for a moment, then took my hand and led me into one of the guest bedrooms. We undressed and caressed each other. I could feel her wanting me, but just when I was about to enter her, she told me to stop. She was not taking the pill, she said, because she hated the side effects. Anyway, she added, she only wanted to be penetrated when she was drunk or tripping. I offered to get her a drink, but she refused. Alcohol made her sick, she said. We continued making love. She was still aroused, but when I asked her if I could enter her, she said she didn't want to come. She insisted that I wouldn't like what happened to her after she came, that she cried and screamed. I kissed her eyes, her hair, her mouth and told her how much I wanted to feel myself inside her. Again she resisted, saying that she didn't need to have an orgasm in order to like me. My fingers played with her flesh and I kissed and sucked her again. Her body twisted and quivered, she was panting and very wet, but she did not come. She pushed me away from her and began to sob. I tried to hold her but she pulled back, covering her face with a pillow and weeping uncontrollably. After she quieted down, I put my arms around her and asked why she hadn't come. She said nothing, but after a moment she told me she often locked herself in her room and aroused herself by fantasizing or reading erotic literature. She would lie on her stomach caressing herself until she came. I asked her if she had ever had an orgasm with a man. A few days before, she said, she had taken LSD with an African student who was anxious to try acid for the first time. They had gone to his room, where they screwed while they were tripping. His sweat was oily and smelled sour, and she noticed he wasn't circumcised. While he was on top of her, she saw him as a glistening black animal, half-lizard, half-squirrel, eating his way deep into her. She didn't have the strength to throw him off and he came inside her. Afterwards she was terrified about getting pregnant. She went to the health service, told them she had been raped and asked for a "morning after" pill.

I stretched out on my back and forced her head down between my thighs. "Do it," I ordered her. "I don't care how you feel about it. I want you to make me come." I kept her pinned down, and she obeyed. She lowered her head and drew me into her mouth. I told her she was too gentle and pressed her head even lower as if to smother her. She moved up and down methodically exciting me with her hands as well as her tongue. I could tell she was aroused again. She kept working on me, swaying back and forth and almost losing her balance, but when she felt that I was about to come, she stopped, pulled back and hid her face in the pillow. She did not cry.

I have given Karen my notes and the photographs from Burma, India and Africa. I gave them to her because I wanted to show her something tangible from my past to make her understand it. At the same time I wonder what this new knowledge about me will mean to her. I am always afraid that some incident from my past will destroy other people's affection for me. Since I have no idea exactly what that incident will be, I have learned to be defensive. I have become a master of the art of concealment, of tailoring my reminiscences to the person I'm talking to. Generally this means suppressing anything that might conceivably sound nauseating or foul. But with Karen I'm not so frightened. With her there is no need to hide those things in me that seem bizarre or ugly.

This is an important change for me. With other people I've always had to be cautious. My friends could never understand my ambivalence towards life. They thought I was continually drifting in and out of situations, trying to escape from myself and my family. They did not understand that I was pushing myself to extremes in order to discover my many selves. If I had revealed too much, they would have reacted with horror. Or, worse, they would have "accepted" me, viewing my attitude towards life as eccentricity and my interests as aberrations.

Only once before have I experienced the freedom I feel with Karen. It was during those months in Africa with Anne, although Anne was never as close to me as Karen has become. She didn't reach me sexually the way Karen does. The possibility of becoming close to Karen is more exciting than anything else has ever been. I begin to feel that I could be loved for whatever I am, not for my actions or my appearance. Everything about me would be acceptable; everything would be a reflection of my central self. I'm sure there are aspects of my personality buried within me that will surface as soon as I know I am completely loved.

When I gave Karen the notes, I told her I had written them for myself. Perhaps I even believed it. No doubt it made me uneasy to think I had not written those words purely for my own gratification. Yet I must have known that Karen would read them. I must have known that someday they would belong to her.

There's a place beyond words where experience first

occurs to which I always want to return. I suspect that whenever I articulate my thoughts or translate my impulses into words, I am betraying the real thoughts and impulses which remain hidden. Instead of expressing myself, I produce a neatly ordered document about someone else's state of mind.

As I find myself mentally reviewing my notes I wish they were more complete. What if Karen finds my perception of her inadequate? Perhaps she will ridicule me for being naïve and banal. I regret having made myself so accessible.

The struggle within me was so great that I was sweating from the tension. It was as if a physical contest was going on between the two halves of myself. One moment I was speaking in a controlled voice, the next moment I was a child, screaming, "How could she have said that? How can all of you avoid seeing what she is doing?" I wanted everyone else to see that her words were tearing me apart, but no one noticed. A fat woman was telling me about her yacht. I saw her lips move, but inside me I heard only Karen's voice: "I am going to forget you. Ours will be the only relationship I won't remember." I accepted a canapé and sipped my Scotch.

As a child I used to lie on the floor with my eyes tightly closed and hope that people would walk past without noticing me. That would mean I was truly invisible. Yet I remember my anxiety when my father's valet, Anthony, once did walk by without stopping. Clearly I wanted to be seen. Now I discover that I have always been more than visible. I have been continually watched. Because of my father, the Company and the money, people have always been employed to make sure of my existence. My father was the only one who acted as though I didn't exist.

I have never been able to lose myself. If one self failed, another was always ready to take its place. Once I sat crouched in a chair staring at the mirror in the living room. My whole face seemed to glow: I was weak and childlike. Suddenly I sat up and my face became totally expressionless. I had no control over the change. It simply happened. Another time I hid behind my father's filing cabinet and screamed at the top of my lungs. I planned to continue for hours—until someone found me. Then I heard voices and stopped. "Someone screamed," said my father; my mother replied: "No one screamed. We're late, let's go." I opened my mouth to scream again, but I couldn't.

When Karen mocks and attacks me, she unlocks the child within me. I am terrified by anxiety and loneliness and I feel myself fragmenting into a jumble of furious emotions. It is like a short, intense sickness. I wait paralyzed until the pieces inside the kaleidoscope settle back into their proper places and I become a unit once again.

.

I still suffer from my father's rejection and my mother's indifference. Yet I know that I am wrong to accept this unjustified and self-inflicted pain. I deserve no punishment at all for being who I am.

Karen and I argue about the encounter group. I tell her that in order to be honest I must always play a number of roles at once. When I play my father, I must speak in the voice that punishes me. Yet that condemning voice is also the voice which comforts me saying: "Because you are my son, you are safe and better than others." The roles overlap like a cover which protects a child but which may at the same time suffocate and destroy him. Karen says I'm lying.

I feel my old fear of violence returning. It began in early childhood when I lay in bed and listened to my father rage. I couldn't bear it and I think everyone, including my mother, felt the same way. Those few times I dared to disagree with him, he struck me even if my nanny was around. He also took out his fury on my dog, Mesabi. One night in Watch Hill, I woke to Mesabi's yelping. I put on my bathrobe and went down to the beach. My father stood at the water's edge, grasping the dog by the collar and punching its head and ribs with his fist. The dog howled with pain. I did not interfere. I simply watched, torn by pity for the dog, anger at my father and hatred for my own weakness. In defense I learned to retreat to a world of fantasies in which I was always the victor. I played with toy soldiers and sharp knives. I read books about great leaders and I made them my heroes. I remember how pleased I was that their biographies never mentioned parents. These men seemed to have been born without fathers; no wonder they had always been strong and powerful, able to mete out punishment whenever they pleased. They were born fathers.

When we were adolescents, Karen and I began to discover sex together. We told each other our families' nicknames for genitals, "Titi" and "little ugly sofky." She wanted to know where my "little ugly sofky" went when I cycled. Did it lie along the top of the bicycle saddle or fall down one side? Did it get squashed when I lay on my stomach? One afternoon when we were in the woods with some other children, we experimented with branches. Karen can still remember how the branch felt going deep inside her, and how afraid she was to scream. One of the girls told Karen's mother about the episode in the woods. Her mother spanked her and took away a fifty-cent piece I had given her, saying it was dirty money from dirty boys who did dirty things to her in the woods.

I remember Karen's touching me. We called it my

"bobolink," and she tried to snatch it away from me. She claimed that women's nipples were permanently stiff. I couldn't imagine it. A few years later, when I saw a stripper for the first time, what I really wanted to see were her nipples. They seemed hard.

When we were older, we talked about finger-fucking. Karen said if a guy is making it with a girl and she really doesn't know how far she wants to go, and then begins to be afraid and draws the line, that's one thing. But it's another when girls set out to get finger-fucked and nothing more. I asked her if it hurts the first time. She said that getting screwed is what hurts. She told me how embarrassed and frightened she was that first night we parked near the beach. But, she said, as soon as she felt my fingers inside her she relaxed and felt only pleasure.

Suppose some average girl doesn't want to get laid by a particular guy. Would she still want him to finger her? "Why not?" Karen answered. "If a girl can get an orgasm out of it she doesn't need any real fucking." I wondered then whether a girl could have an orgasm simply from finger-fucking. I doubted it.

One day when Karen had just drunk a glass of straight vodka, she said, "You're hiding something." She smiled. "You're hiding a dead body. Your own."

It ended there. From then until I went abroad we had no contact with each other. Why hadn't she provoked me? I wondered. Why hadn't she gotten openly angry or frustrated instead of insulting me? Everything in her suddenly seemed premeditated and dull. She had no spontaneity, no imagination. She seemed imperturbable, as if she existed in a vacuum. She had infected me. I had already begun to exist with the same deadness, the same unwillingness to react.

Why do I always choose women who cannot give of themselves, whose concept of love is based on repression and undeclared competition? I see a ludicrous picture: It is after midnight; grey-haired Jonathan James Whalen sits in his library. That afternoon he has confessed to his psychiatrist that he has never lost to a woman, that he has always established control over women. While Whalen sits at his desk, the woman he desires lies in his bed, unattended.

What I want is tangible proof that I matter to Karen. I get it only in negative ways. Yesterday at her party I was talking with an editor from a beauty magazine. She said, "I'm going to stay away from you because otherwise everyone will think you're fucking me." About an hour later she brushed past me in the hall and said, "I'd like you to come to my apartment. But what if I never let you leave?" She didn't attract me at all, but I liked the idea that I attracted her. As I kissed her, Karen walked in.

The guests wouldn't leave. Until two in the morning we drank beer and told stories. Karen ignored me the entire time. When everyone else had finally left, she turned to me and said: "Go ahead, fuck the editor bitch, go ahead and fuck her. Just leave me alone!"

We went to bed. I was confident that I could change her mood and began to kiss her. She sat up and slapped my face. "Cut it out," she shouted, "or I'll slap the hell out of you! Now let me sleep." I felt humiliated, yet at that moment my desire was much stronger than it had been before.

On the phone the next day she said she didn't want to continue anything with me since I had something going with someone else. I lied and told her she was right. She asked if I was in love with the girl. I said, "No, but I'm not detached. It's impossible for me to screw and remain detached. To be with a woman, to be inside her, to have her all over me—" I went on and on. Then Karen apologized by saying that she had been hysterical when she hit me. She hadn't really meant it. I found myself remembering that whore who had hit me with her purse when I told her she was asking too much money. I was immediately hers. In her tough fuck-the-world way, she gained control of me as a compliant woman never could.

Before I left America there were other men around Karen; particularly there was David. His being an actor gave him a larger-than-life, star quality: Stick your dick out the window and screw them all, on the table, on the carpet, against a wall, hump and jump and kick and lick— that was David. Once, in front of me, Karen said to him, "I would like to fuck you, baby, until, until—" Then she dragged him into the bathroom and slammed the door. When she came out, she said to him, "Will I see you again?" and he answered, "I don't know. That depends on how bad you want it."

To help me with my affairs the bank provided me with a secretary, a slight timid girl with thick glasses and no make-up. Walking down the street this hot sticky after-

41

noon I find myself at a loss, wanting to invite her in, yet not wanting to and not knowing how to anyway. Did Karen ever feel shy and ambivalent on the nights when she betrayed me?

When we were lying next to each other, Karen said that now that she was liberated, she could understand me better. My biggest hang-ups, she said, were my lack of spontaneity, my steadiness and my unyielding self-control. I told her it wasn't any help knowing she could read or fall asleep so easily while I stayed awake and tense. She slid her hand along the inside of my thigh and when I didn't react she turned away and said, "Good night, ice cube, maybe we'll clink against each other during the night." It was as though she had totally forgotten how many times she had turned me down, as though she weren't the most self-controlled woman I had ever known. She fell asleep while I was telling her this. It was just perfect.

You might be pleased to know, Jonathan, that this week two of your former trustees have been called to high posts in Washington. James Abbott has been chosen to be Assistant Secretary for European Affairs; and our former chairman, Charles Sothern, has been nominated by the President to be Secretary of the Treasury. Other members of the board have also had changes in their lives. Walter William Howmet, your father's closest assistant, has reached compulsory retirement age. However, he has graciously agreed to stay on as an honorary board member. Stanley Kenneth Clavin, another member of the board, has decided to retire from his post as chief executive officer of the Company. Mr. Clavin says that with younger leadership emerging in almost every major division of the Company, the new management should be free to work as a team.

A toothless old black man, unmistakably an addict, was sitting across from me on the subway. As two young policemen got on he winked and mumbled, "I feel so good here, son, so good. You protect me." He rocked back and forth, attracting the policemen's attention. One of them came over and told him to get off at the next stop. "I'm just going home," he protested, "going home." When the doors opened at the next stop and the man didn't move, the policemen shoved him off the train. It was my stop, so I got off and followed them along the platform. The policemen jostled the man and he fell to the pavement, insisting he couldn't get up again. The policemen grabbed him by the arms and dragged him along the platform. His shoe fell off. One of the cops snatched it with the end of his night stick and threw it onto the track. Only then the policemen noticed that I was following them and demanded to know what I wanted. "What did he do?" I asked. "He threatened me with his cane," said one of them, smiling. Without a word I went off in the opposite direction to find another witness. When I returned, the policemen were gone. The old man lay on his back, his face smeared with tears and blood.

I helped him to his feet and told him to go home but he wouldn't move. "No," he cried. "They won't let me, they be waitin' for me." When I had walked up the stairs I looked back at him. He had sunk to his knees on the platform, and was rocking back and forth again, staring at the blood on his hands.

I tell you, Mr. Whalen, some people are really amazing. I mean like there she was putting the make on this guy right here in the cemetery. Since I started working around here, you know, I've seen a lot of different people with a lot of different feelings but she was just plain horny. And there she was, I don't know, about twenty, beautiful long blond hair. With this dude about twenty-five, maybe not even that. She sure wasn't mourning, let me tell you. She was giggling, and pretty soon he was giggling too. And then right there, maybe two hundred yards from your father's grave, he's got one hand on her tits and the other one on her crotch. I couldn't believe it. Like it was really sexy seeing this chick worked up, you know? I mean she wasn't exactly fighting him off. I kept wondering what those boobs felt like, you know, and if these kids were going to make it just like that on somebody's grave. Me, I felt like jerking off right then and there.

My servant in Calcutta did everything for me, from answering my mail to starting the car on rainy mornings. He cooked my dinner and accompanied me everywhere. I

45

panicked when he quit, but after he was gone I didn't hire another servant. I have never missed anyone for very long, no matter how much I suffered at their actual departure.

I take good care of myself. I am well organized and at least during the last week I have managed all the superficial details of my life in an orderly fashion. I eat good food in the best restaurants; I even went to the dentist. I note all my appointments on my calendar, make lists of things to do and to buy and neatly cross off my accomplished chores.

I have talked to lawyers about my income and my taxes and settled the questions of who will manage my affairs and how the bank will pay my bills from now on. I have learned where in the bank vault my major financial documents are kept. I have even arranged my clothes in the hotel closet so they all face the same way.

I think it would be particularly hard to live with Karen, because she demands so much from herself and others. She insists on working despite the fact that with my income she wouldn't have to. She needs me to be "fatherly" but I can't. Whether or not Karen wants a person like Susan, she definitely needs someone like her—reliable, utterly dependable and faithful—and I am unable to meet that need.

Anne played the same role with me that Susan plays with Karen. But there was one important difference: Anne had been in analysis for many years and understood my defenses very well. She had seen me out of control, had put up with me even when I was manipulative and cruel towards her. She empathized with my fear, my self-doubt and rage. I was destructive towards her, yet she tried to help me.

Anne suffered when I began to see Maria, because she realized she couldn't possibly compete with her. She knew me well enough to recognize that I could become very attached to Maria and that Maria could relieve me in ways that she could not. But she did not protest. She accepted her torment with complete passivity. I also lied to Maria about Anne. I said our relationship was something I had to work out, but that I was tired of Anne and would leave her soon. Yet even after I had supposedly left Anne, I continued to see her.

I dreamed last night that Susan, Karen and I were staying in a huge house filled with people. Karen was busy organizing everything, and I was shy, useless and terribly lonely. Karen was able to run the house and organize things all by herself; I could only stand in a corner of the room and watch. This made Susan very happy.

I notice I never feel sympathetic towards Karen when she is exhausted or doesn't feel well. I am tired of her excuses. Several times when I've been at the bank, surrounded by people who are obviously eavesdropping, she's called at noon to say that she can't see me in the evening. Under the circumstances, I couldn't freely express my indignation on the phone. Twice before, I had been looking forward to spending a couple of pleasant days with her after a grueling week of business and both times she called it off only a few hours before she was supposed to arrive. I am afraid her erratic behavior is becoming habitual. It suggests that other people and events are more important to her than I am. I am afraid that her canceling plans means she no longer cares about me and that she will eventually end the relationship. Of course if she really needs rest, she shouldn't see me, but are our visits always going to be so exhausting that we can see each other only when we are both well rested? Will we meet and then go back into our private lives to recuperate? Karen may be legitimately tired, but there is obviously much more to it than that. If only she had said, "I just don't feel up to being with you this weekend," I would have accepted it much more easily. Yesterday when she called I made sure that I was completely unresponsive. I knew that was destructive, that I should have released my anger, but there are still dark areas of doubt and mistrust in my life. Karen's resistance sets off explosions within me. I become totally vulnerable, and when I feel the least bit insecure, I instinctively retreat into sarcasm. It's like skin-diving. There is serenity and calm under the water's surface. You move easily and glimpse a world you have never seen before. You think of running out of oxygen and the idea of sharks darts out at you. You sense that there is something treacherous hiding behind every reef; no matter how much you explore you won't ever know what it is.

I traveled as your mother's nurse only once. I was vacationing with my family at their home in the south of Italy when your mother's doctor telephoned from New Haven and asked me to interrupt my holiday and join her right away. Apparently your mother had radioed him during the night, and he could tell that an attack was imminent. The boat was two days away from the nearest airport, and she was too sick to be moved. A plane was sent to pick me up at the local airport and fly me to Madrid. From Madrid the American consul arranged for a U.S. Army helicopter to ferry me to your mother's yacht at Formentera.

When I arrived, your mother was already in a bad state. She was furious that I had come and wanted the helicopter recalled to take me away again. She ordered the crew to detain me in a cabin. I showed the captain, who was Spanish, my instructions and the injections and medications I'd brought with me, but he refused to be reasonable. Apparently just before I had arrived, one of your mother's guests, a middle-aged man, had given one of the sailors a narcotic. While the teen-aged boy was under the influence of the drug, the guest violated him. The boy was found in a cabin, bleeding badly and hallucinating from the drug. The captain asked your mother to make her guest pay damages to the boy and did his best to keep the affair quiet. Because of this, your mother became even more difficult and demanded that I leave the ship. Even though they realized how sick she was, most of her guests pretended to take her side. When I didn't leave, your mother became hysterical. She locked herself in her cabin, refusing to see anyone. From outside, we could hear her throwing things around the room. I tried to persuade her to come out, but she wouldn't, and the captain refused to have the door opened. Meanwhile a storm blew up. To avoid the yacht's dragging its anchor, we left the harbor and made for the open sea, which was already rough. At last I persuaded the captain to force the cabin door. As soon as it was pushed in, your mother began screaming. She wouldn't let me close enough to give her an injection. I had been warned by the doctor that this had happened many times before, but I hadn't realized that I would need assistance.

When I tried to approach her, your mother picked up a marble letter opener and threatened to stab me. She began hurling hairbrushes, make-up bottles, brooches, pendants, rings, anything she could find. Some objects fell out the open portholes, but most of them just bounced off the wall and landed on the floor.

By the time the captain closed the portholes, several valuable pieces of jewelry had been thrown out into the sea. Only then did it occur to him that your mother's condition was serious. He must have realized that the jewelry was valuable and that he and his crew might be liable for it.

Eventually your mother calmed down. She was pale and very weak, and her body was bruised from many falls during rough weather. She began to tremble and vomit. Like a sick child she asked for help, and when I went to her, she didn't fight me. An empty bottle of prescription drugs was lying close to some half-empty gin and vodka bottles. The captain was worried. He radioed the U.S. consul. The same helicopter which brought me to the boat was now waiting for us in the port. In Palma I packed your mother's belongings—I remember a photograph of you with your father was among them—and helped carry her to the plane. We flew to Madrid, where a chartered jet was waiting to take us to the States. During the flight your mother was given preliminary treatment and fed intravenously. A limousine met us at the airport and took us to the New Haven hospital. Two days later I returned to Italy to continue my vacation.

It's like operating any big gadget. Gliders are just big fiberglass ballast tanks equipped with all kinds of instruments. You squeeze yourself inside the cockpit and lean way back like a racing-car driver. You learn which levers are for flaps, which for gear retraction, for tow release, and for the landing parachute. There are also an altimeter, compass, oxygen gauge, and so forth. It's not as complicated as it sounds.

When you first get going behind the tow, your speed increases slowly. You feel like a heavy bird which can't quite make it into the air. Then, when you are only a few feet off the ground, the wings bend up on their ends like a bow and the fuselage is slowly lifted into the air. Finally you pull the tow release and take up the landing gear. All you hear is the wind, and all you see are clouds puffed up around you like cotton balls.

It's quite a feeling when you hit around one hundred and forty miles an hour. You swoop up and down, and the clouds swirl as you rush towards them. The whole plane trembles. Then you nose up and everything's peaceful again. But most of all you love the speed, which at any moment could shake you apart.

I met him the first time at the sand-yacht race in Africa. The yachts were slender, delicate structures with bright sails and three small rubber wheels. In a strong wind, their sails tightened and strained and the yachts took off, as if catapulted from a slingshot, speeding down the hard-packed beach and soon becoming pale dots of color dissolving in the heat.

They raced on a large strip of sandy Ukunda beach along the ocean and the jungle. As they reached the far end of the beach, they tacked against the wind, cutting diagonally across from the jungle to the ocean, turned just at the edge of the water, one wheel grazing the shallows, the other straight up in the air. Then they raced at the green wall of the jungle, turning as one wheel scraped the shriveled roots of the trees, and sped back to the ocean. Just before the finish, one of the racers lost control during a sharp turn. His yacht overturned and smashed. One wheel broke off and rolled into the jungle, striking a huge snake wrapped around a tree trunk. The thin wooden ribs of the cockpit pierced the man's chest and his blood seeped into the sand and yellow sail, drying instantly. The snake slithered across the beach, circled the wreck, then coiled itself around the broken mast.

A European racer on his way overland to Lesotho agreed to let me join him. We took off in an old Toyota for Dar es Salaam, but at dusk we left the roadway and drove through narrow jungle trails towards the ocean. In the rapidly descending dark our headlights picked up the glowing eyes of the prowling jungle cats. We stopped on the beach when the sand was still warm and stretched out our blankets beside the car, leaving the radio playing to frighten off animals.

Just before retiring, the racer turned on the bright carbide lamp, opened a small plastic bag and removed a bottle of isopropyl alcohol, a thin glass vial, a tiny disposable syringe and some cotton pads. I watched him disinfect his left forearm and fill the syringe with the white fluid from the vial. He ran the short needle carefully up under the skin's surface to avoid piercing the narrow veins and slowly injected the fluid into his arm. He explained that the injection was to counteract an eye virus which attacks the optic nerve and can cause blindness without warning. Since there is no known remedy strong enough to kill the virus without severely damaging the eye itself, he'd had an autogenous vaccine made of his virus for self-administration. The virus was deadly, and the vaccine had been prepared at his own risk. When I asked what risk it involved, he answered casually that if his body should not be able to reject the vaccine's poison he would die. He said he was increasing the dosage weekly with the hope that, while his body rejected the vaccine, his eyes would also develop enough resistance to combat and reject it. "How many of these injections have you already given yourself?" I asked. He watched the growing redness on his arm. "Three. But this time I increased the dosage significantly." I was horrified by the prospect of being left in the jungle with his dead body seventy miles from any human settlement.

"Don't you think," I said, "that you should be somewhere near a hospital, or at least near a doctor?" "I do not," he said. "It wouldn't matter, because there's no antidote for the virus. It would be as though I were bitten by a venomous snake. In a few minutes my jaw would lock, my eyelids refuse to open and my lungs stop taking in oxygen." He looked at his watch. "Five minutes," he remarked, replacing the vial in the bag, "and I can still open my eyes. I guess I won't die from it this week."

"How many weeks of injections do you need?"

"About fifty unless I go blind before that," he answered. "But I could be bitten by a lethal snake while I'm sleeping. Good night." He extinguished the lamp and fell asleep. I lay listening to the jungle noises, thinking of the snake looped around the mast.

Next day as we drove through the dense underbrush he pointed to a couple of native children quite far from the village compound. "Many children are kidnapped here," he said. "Deviates and poachers come from all over Europe to Africa, rent a safari vehicle and take solitary tours off the main road where they can grab an unsuspecting African girl or boy. They violate the child as they please, kill it and drop the body into the bush, where it is often devoured by animals."

Later I asked, "Why do you know this jungle so well?"

"I like children," he answered, laughing.

"You might recall that these debentures became part of your holdings when the trustees decided to sell your interest in Tinplate to S.F.I. Would you be willing to tender all or part of them for common stock? The income would be less but the stock would represent a more attractive growth investment. The offer would be 3.2 shares of S.F.I. common for each one hundred dollars of debenture value. This would represent about seventy-five dollars' worth of common stock for debentures that sold recently at sixty-eight dollars and earlier this year for as little as fifty-three dollars. Of course whether the other debenture holders will accept such an offer depends on the optimism about S.F.I.'s market strength. As you may know, its shares have moved extremely well lately, and that means that there is a risk of profit-taking by the common-stock shareholders. If all the debentures were to be tendered, S.F.I.'s balance sheet would certainly look a good deal better, with its debt decreased and its equity increased. Additionally, the number of S.F.I. shares outstanding would increase almost three times, and much of the leverage, which made the stock so attractive to begin with, would be lost. It is a question of balancing the gains against the risks—"

"When do you need my answer?" asked Whalen.

"The advantage of your situation is that there is no pressure on you to decide. However, since you are the majority stockholder your eventual position will have to be determined—"

"I understand," said Whalen. "Let me think about it."

"Certainly. Certainly. Our financial and legal departments will gladly assist you at any time. Just call my office and they—"

"There's something I would like to know."

"Yes?"

"Who is the Company's second majority shareholder?"

"Mr. Howmet. At one time he was a close friend of your father and sat on the board of his Company. Later there seems to have been a difference of opinion between them. Recently Howmet left our Company—or, rather, retired. But he will continue to keep an eye on our policies, and as a shareholder will work to influence them. Perhaps you would like to meet the Howmets?"

"I already have. They are my godparents."

Whenever I stand near a window high up in a tall building I have a recurrent desire to put my head through it. I imagine every detail in slow motion: the glass cracks and splinters, shattering its reflections. I see my blood and hear the glass hitting the sidewalk and the roofs of cars and the screams of people far below.

About two months before my return to America, Jack's wife was committed to a mental hospital. He was lonely and needed to talk, so this morning he came to my hotel. I was surprised that he wanted to confide in me.

His wife, he said, had always suffered from an over-whelming sense of unworthiness and an obsessive fear of rejection. When I asked him how she had ever managed to overcome her fears and become his wife, he said he had forced the issue; he had demanded she marry him. Throughout our conversation an unstated question was forming in my mind: How could he still have wanted to marry her after she admitted all her fears and weaknesses to him? I began to see that he loved her in spite of her self-contempt; he simply ignored her perception of herself and created his own vision of her. It occurred to me that I could never love like that, nor could I respect anyone who didn't share my perception of myself. I have always suspected everyone who likes me of having poor judgment. I despise them for being so easily taken in.

I want to retreat. During the last few days I have fallen back into self-hatred. One more uncontrollable attempt to destroy my peace and stability. I feel that I will never be able to carry anything off, and my independence, my inheritance, my relationship with Karen all demand so much responsibility. I still dread the thought of anyone being important to me. Before I came back to America, I was resigned to being alone. But now that things have changed, I cannot go back to Burma or Africa for a while, even though the possibility makes me feel more comfortable here at home.

Karen once said that psychotherapy is like treatment for a broken shinbone that mended crookedly. It must be broken again and set properly.

But in psychotherapy there is no anesthesia, no clearly defined period of healing, no assurance that things will mend. For a while the new walk seems like a limp to you and to those who know you. With a shinbone, the second break is worse, because you can anticipate the pain. But you cannot anticipate the pain of psychotherapy or the new gait it will give you. Except that your imagination is free to toy with terrifying possibilities.

The other day I saw a film in which people were shot in the face time and time again, and at one point a fountain of blood bubbled up from a woman's mouth. In another scene one man hit a woman with a bull whip, then pressed his mouth to the wound and drew away with blood on his lips. Even though I knew that it was only red dye, I flinched. I tried to force myself to see the end of the film but couldn't. I have had too many traumatic experiences with blood. What if they had been nothing more than strong reactions to red dye?

Last night I dreamed I was in Africa, knowing that my mother was ill and hoping that my trip would be her punishment for giving birth to a child who was not to fulfill his father's dreams.

It was over a hundred and fifty years ago, Richard said, that the mentally ill were first taught to suppress the signs of their illness for the benefit of the sane. Patients were made conscious of the visible symptoms of their madness, and forced to conceal or overcome their morbid propensities. Madmen, it was assumed, were capable of some self-control. To prove this, the asylum doctors often took their patients to town and to religious meetings, where they were made to behave like normal people. Madness couldn't be understood or cured, but could at least be made socially acceptable.

Today it's worse, Richard said. Our mentally ill and

retarded are excluded from national health and medical-aid programs as if they were not sick and disabled. Millions of people who need care remain unseen, locked in attics, chained in basements or seated in front of TV sets so that they'll be presentable to neighbors who drop in for coffee.

Richard feels that in his own psychoanalysis he is being treated like these madmen, that the whole process is intended to make life easier for others, rather than for him. All therapy, from individual analysis to group encounters, is designed to make disturbed patients conform, rather than allow them to discover and live by their individual emotional truths.

At his supermarket Richard noticed that the stand with fresh fruits, salad greens and vegetables was placed next to a large display of garden insecticides and bug repellents, many labeled "hazardous if swallowed." Richard approached the shop's manager and told him that someone might spray the fruits and vegetables with these poisons without anyone's noticing it. The manager, an older Jewish man, was astonished.

"Why would anyone want to poison the fruits?" he asked in his heavy Eastern European accent. "What for?"

"Because they are next to the poisons, that's why," answered Richard.

"You must be nuts," said the man, moving away. Richard cornered him and said, "You are a Jew. Millions of your people died poisoned by gas. Why would anyone kill Jews?"

Richard, whose few surviving relatives came to this country from White Russia, told me that in Nazi-occupied territories during World War II, Jews, lunatics and the infectiously ill were the first to be massacred in savage outdoor executions, which took place frequently until the gas chambers were established.

I asked Karen what her life was like when I was away. "I remember so many weekends, one just like the next," she said. "At dinner, whatever man I was with would help himself to the food first and talk too loud. Then he would suggest that I have some champagne with him on his boat. I would smile sweetly and say: 'Fine, but I'm not going to bed with you.' I hate slick seduction scenes. In East Hampton, I drank iced mint tea, ate sherbet, and smoked hashish. I dated one handsome son of a bitch whose teeth were like porcelain. When he smiled, people put on their sunglasses. On the back of the photograph he gave me was written: 'Sean, age 27, no make-up, just naturally perfect.' He had grown up in a shack in West Virginia. His family didn't have an indoor toilet till he was eighteen. When he left home at nineteen, he broke his father's heart. When he was twenty-two and in Vietnam he had an affair with a forty-year-old nurse. She liked sex, and there wasn't anybody else around. But then she decided to marry some guy, so they stopped fucking and became friends. He had an older sister he really admired. He stayed with her for a week, but one night his sister's husband threw him out. According to Sean, the husband wanted to make it with him, but he refused to betray his sister. One day he said to me, 'Let's face it. I may not be too smart but my prick is bigger than the average American's. I'm the best goddamn football coach this side of the Mississippi. And the best fuck too.' " Then Karen got down to what she really wanted to tell me. "His direct approach really worked with me," she said. "I always want to give in when a man acts as if he'll do whatever he wants with me. Some women don't like men who treat them with respect. Just before you got back I had a date with a guy who was superliberated. He kept rapping about how sad it was that men depersonalize women and make us into playthings. Finally I couldn't stand it any more. I told him, 'I can't help it if I don't turn you on. Just tell me if I don't. But if I do, for God's sake don't give me all this crap. Just take me to bed.' " She paused. "When you first went away, Jonathan, I wondered whether or not I should screw and if I would actually get around to doing it. I knew I was vulnerable, so I tried to be cautious and rational. I'd heard about women getting fucked over by sex without love. After a few affairs, I tried to avoid having sex because it drained me. I told myself that I was frustrated, not by conventional morality, but because my emotional needs were too strong. I used to worry about being promiscuous until I realized that it was utterly impossible. How many men am I attracted to each year? Ten, fifteen, twenty? If I choose one, the others won't be around. With the average affair lasting three or four months, I actually have only three or four lovers a year. And I say to myself: 'I like him, I desire him, I can imagine the touch of his skin and of his muscles, breathing his breath and feeling him inside me.' This is a straightforward desire, with no pretenses beforehand or regrets afterwards. What could possibly stand in the way of it?"

When Karen spoke again her voice was low and husky. "Our knowing each other again, Jonathan, might lead to something good. But I think it's too soon for me. I ended a relationship just before you got back. Things could develop. If they don't, so what? We haven't deceived each other. We've promised to be together only as long as it's good. I'm sick of my friends who suck guys off in parked cars because it's trendy. I'm tired of sexual fads."

I asked her if she smoked often. "I like to do grass and

hash oil. I get stoned a lot with Susan," she said, "not because it dispels my inhibitions, but because it gives me something to blame things on later. I'm still afraid of freaking out. Remember the African guy in school? For me, sex is like walking in the hills. Each time you reach the top of a hill you see another one just ahead, and you think that's the top and then you see still another one, so you keep climbing, never knowing where the last one will be.

"I often have this nightmare. I hear a man's voice coaxing and urging me and I suddenly freeze and say: 'It isn't fair. You're taking advantage of me.' I feel like screaming, but then I think, what the hell, I need it and I want it, so why not? Still, I can't come. It's emotional, I know, but what can I do about it? Sometimes when the sex is very good, I feel intense pleasure, but I never reach the final hill. I stay detached." Karen got up and wandered around the room, talking on and on as if I weren't there.

" 'You're the hottest lay I've ever had,' a man says, and I think to myself how familiar his act is. Afterwards, when he's not high any more, and he says it again, I feel less afraid. 'Your body's built for sex and you know how to use it; most women just lie there. I can't believe you don't do it all the time. Tell me, has a guy ever come the minute he got inside you?' 'Of course,' I answer. 'I'm not surprised, not at all surprised. You've got the tightest box in the world.'

"In the kitchen, I'm mixing drinks and putting him on about his other women. He says, 'I know a good thing when I see it, and you're very, very good. With a body like that, you won't ever have to work an eight-hour day in any office.'

"After we make love, a man says, 'Fuck it, I'm not going to worry about being cool. I want to tell you it's never been this good for me before. You don't mind being told, do you?' 'Mind?' I say. 'I love it. Who needs that cool Second Avenue body-exchange pick-up crap in bed?' "

Karen looked at me pensively, then continued. "It isn't a mistake to tell you this, is it, Jonathan? I tell myself that it's all right if I don't love you, but I can't stand your not loving me, because then I don't have any power over you. I can dig making it with a man I don't love but not with one who doesn't love me. In a way I didn't want you to be in love with me because it would interfere with my life with Susan and make things awkward for everyone. But I need your love. I'm terrified of being taken lightly."

Later that night, she mentioned a letter I sent her from Kusadasi. "You wrote that Turks are supposed to be the best lovers. You said that they satisfy their women because they don't lose themselves in them and that what excites a Turk is that he can completely manipulate a woman's body and her desire. Why did you write me that?"

My impulse is not to speak or write, but to remain elusive, to present Karen with cartoons of my fears and sexual desires rather than my real ones. But her own elusiveness makes this impossible: she intimidates me into talking frankly. Like her, I would prefer to remain oblique, to avoid making any decision about our future until some crisis arises that compels us to define our commitment. But I am afraid that by our mutual silence we will both lose by default, with neither of us claiming victory over the other, and each going our separate way.

"Don't I have a nice ass and nice tits?" she asked when she arrived at my room. I thought, fuck her, or as one of the drunks at the bar had said, "Eat her deep, man, that's her game!" Lying in bed with her, kissing her, I imagined I could taste and smell the other men on her. After she left, I threw up.

When I woke this morning, I knew I wasn't up to meeting with my tax lawyers. I didn't even feel like answering the phone. I lay there recalling the whole conversation with her last night. "Why are you so worried about whether you were good with me? Why should you care what a whore thinks?" I told her she was right, but that ambition is natural to me and that I want to succeed with everyone. I can't stand the idea of being merely an adequate sexual partner, of letting myself be screwed and sucked by any number of anonymous bodies with hard nipples and round asses.

"Anonymous?" she almost shrieked. "You don't know what anonymous means. Do you know what it's like to go down on stinking men just to keep a lousy modeling job? If only they would say at the start, 'We'll pay you five hundred and fifty dollars a week to blow us and on the side you can be a star!' That wouldn't be as bad. Women should have double cunts: one for business and one for pleasure. At least in this city they should." I didn't feel like talking and so she took advantage of the situation to tell me her troubles, beginning with her first business blow job. The personal manager of a television actor had called her from Los Angeles and said he was going to fly to New York to meet her. She was so perfect on paper that he wanted to see her in person. "You could be the best in the business," he told her, "and I want to hire you, but my boss thinks you're too straight." Later he called to say that he couldn't make it but the actor was arriving in New York on business that evening. Wouldn't she give him a call and suggest a drink? "Baby," the manager said, "you can wrap this thing up. In one evening, you can wrap it up." So there it was. All she had to do to get a job with the actor was to go down on him.

It was always the same after that, though not always as direct. First, sex was only hinted at. It began with: "Take off your dress so I can see all of you. I won't touch you and I won't ask you to do anything." Then it was: "You're so gorgeous. I love your smooth skin—or your beautiful figure or your long legs or your wet crotch. I think you could make me come just with your lips, or by letting me feel your pussy." Or else the guy would give instructions: "It's the texture of the tongue. Some girls just can't do it right. Now, bite a bit, kiss the rim. Now, try there, inside, as deep as you can. I said, as deep as you can, baby, don't make me have to ask you again."

With these men thrashing under or above or in front of or behind her, on the couch, on the carpet, in bed, on the chair, on the john, all she thought about was whether she was making a fool of herself. Afterwards, she would often cry, drying her tears with her hair. She hated herself for even remembering those men. Fucking them

70

humiliated her but she kept on doing it, which made her feel even worse. She always said the same thing to everyone, which depressed her more than fucking them, blowing them or licking their asses. No one ever noticed that she was repeating sexual clichés as mechanically as she manipulated her body. The men were so stupid they couldn't tell the difference between a good lay and a bad one. She was willing to let them use her, but why did they always do it wrong? Why did they make it disgusting even for themselves? "Can't you see my potential?" she would say. "I'm star material, you asshole. Just look at me. I want you to let me use my skin, my lips, my tongue, my velvet cunt, my ass, front or back, to get it on, not just to follow orders. Can't you see that when I do only what you tell me, it ends by revolting you as much as it disgusts me? We both wind up degraded."

I asked her why she didn't quit.

"To do what? Office work? I can't even write a decent letter. I have no talent any more; I can't even pretend for very long that I enjoy sex.

"I still remember what it was like after the first time. I told the actor's manager about what the actor had made me do. I played the outraged girl: 'Maury doesn't screw. He likes tricks.' He told me Maury was going around saying I gave him the best blow job he'd ever had. 'Which,' the manager said, 'is a pity. Such a good beginning and you wasted all the cream. How about me, kid?' the man-

71

ager said. 'I like you too.' I didn't want to touch him at first because I hadn't washed; I was uneasy even when he kissed my tits. But after twenty minutes or so he really turned me on and I really wanted to fuck with him, perhaps because I was accepted without having to wash. At first he couldn't get it up and my choice was clear: either I get him hard or I go back to a little desk in some office, rent a crummy one-room apartment and live an ordinary little life. I decided: he finally managed to get it up. Then he gave me a whole load of crap about physical, not just sexual, love! He kissed me on the lips and said, 'The best thing about sixty-nine is that our senses are centered in our faces. Our eyes are there, and this way everything can be seen, and seeing is the essence of sex.' He could say this, the stupid bastard, after I ate him with my eyes shut and my jaw aching, about to vomit from his taste.

"I can't be alone for too long," she said. "I wallow and complain and don't do anything for anybody. I'm nowhere. I live only for other people, for looking good and keeping healthy. I do everything to get a reaction. I'm known now—maybe not in the way I wanted to be— but at least people notice me. Men don't know who I am but they remember seeing me in the porno magazines and start following me. From time to time I even enjoy being the way I am. I want money, and I don't really care where it comes from. Eventually I'll probably marry one of them. The madam who sent me here said you're rich, Whalen. Why don't you marry me?"

When I was withdrawing from drugs in Munich, I talked with an American psychiatrist about my guilt feelings from leaving Maria and opium behind. The doctor seemed to think that I was repeating a familiar pattern, once more creating an artificial system of guilt from which there was no escape. As I talked to him I realized that I was concerned less with leaving Maria than with losing contact with her father. I was setting myself up to be judged and condemned by a man whom I respected and to whom I felt curiously close. Since I've returned, I've even considered confiding in him. But I can't really see it happening. He would blame me for breaking up with his daughter. His allegiance would be completely with her.

This morning Karen showed me photographs of us taken just before my departure. I was relieved to see that in the years that have passed, my appearance has altered for the better. When I was a child, I thought my possessions and properties belonged to me because I was pretty, as everyone continually assured me. Now I know I despise people who associate the way I look with my money and family connections, as though physical attractiveness is merely a matter of expensive shirts and custom-made suits. But even now it's hard for me to imagine being very wealthy and ugly at the same time: money and beauty are still my God-given rights.

"Have you ever known a woman who got old without being afraid?" asked Karen. "Have you ever known one who kept faith with herself? This society makes people terrified of aging. Youth is the only commodity you can't buy, even if you're rich, when you're old and repulsive."

I saw Karen's photograph in several old magazines she kept in her apartment and realized that she had been modeling while I was abroad. Karen in swimwear striking sexy poses aroused mixed feelings in me. I was proud of her body, as though I owned it, but I was also hurt that she was so available to everyone. I've felt this conflict before, that night at the East Hampton party, and even more so in the bar on Third Avenue. I'm uneasy when men flock around Karen. In a way I'm glad she's so strongly attracted to Susan, because Susan shields her from other men.

When I was a boy, I introduced my father to some of my friends by saying, "This is my father. He's a business-man, he's very rich, he owns half of this town." Instantly my mother reprimanded me for bragging. I must have read into this event that it was wrong for me to find my father powerful and rich; maybe it was even wrong to like him.

Today during our lunch Susan reminisced about college. It was a women's school, which seemed to turn out only girls who were well-mannered, well-groomed and pleasant to talk to: perfect wives for doctors, lawyers and business-men. Susan said that even though her average college boy friend could accept the fact that his girl was not a virgin, he was still preoccupied with her previous lovers. He usually assumed that his girl friend considered her first lover a mistake and her second merely a test case. As her third lover, he would convince himself that only now, with him, was his woman sexually mature, aware of the flaws in her two previous relationships and ready to settle down.

Susan said that she had dated a man like that for almost two years. Christopher was handsome and he was a brilliant scholar. Towards the end of the second year Susan told him that she had had many lovers. He called her a whore and refused to have anything more to do with her.

A year ago Susan found out that in a few months Christopher was going to defend his doctoral dissertation on medieval miracle plays. She decided to help his career.

She learned that one of the most prominent authorities in the field of medieval theater was a professor at a university on the West Coast. She flew out, posed as a new graduate assistant, got a passkey and entered the professor's office at night. The professor kept his notes neatly typed on small index cards in open files. Susan photographed all his pertinent research, original opinions and theories and then returned the cards to the files.

At home she patiently scribbled the material on various odd sheets of paper and envelopes. Then she sent them to her former boy friend with a letter: "Dear Christopher, I remember that during our college years you were always interested in the medieval period. In case it's still your field, I enclose various notes on the subject left by my uncle, who died last week of cancer of the lungs. In his last few years he became interested in miracle plays. I'm sure he would be pleased to know that his labor was not in vain, and that there is someone who can benefit from his studies. All the very best, Jim." She hoped Christopher would think that the package was sent by someone with whom he'd studied but didn't remember.

After Christopher successfully defended his dissertation, it was filed in the university library. Susan visited the library and compared Christopher's dissertation with her copy of the stolen materials. As she hoped, Christopher had incorporated as his own a major portion of the information she had sent him.

Susan telephoned the West Coast professor and informed him that recently a Ph.D. dissertation had been defended that contained material copied from his files. The professor investigated the charge and demanded a special inquiry at Christopher's university. Christopher could not satisfactorily explain how he had come into possession of the professor's materials. He could not even recall the name of the friend who sent him the notes. He was dismissed from the university and his academic career came to an abrupt end.

I remember Karen insisting that Susan had a very tenuous hold on reality. When they first became close friends and roommates, Susan started picking up Karen's mannerisms and figures of speech until it seemed that she was deliberately imitating her. She dressed like Karen, copied her hair style, took up her interests and even went after men Karen had been with. This continued until they became very close, when Susan seemed self-confident enough to develop her own personality.

Karen suggested that she, Susan and I live together, an ideal solution with no risks for Karen and Susan, but with endless problems for me. How would outsiders view this arrangement? And who would be the most expendable if the threesome failed, as I feel it inevitably would? If anything went wrong, the result would be painful and humiliating for me. That possibility doesn't seem to have crossed Karen's mind. She doesn't want to admit her dependence on Susan and would resent my describing their relationship as dependent. But what is it that the two of them share that I could not share with Karen? Is Susan merely a receptacle for Karen's experiences or does she mold them? I'm not convinced by Karen's explanation that Susan is a marvelous housekeeper and a good companion, completely forgiving and patient. Such companions normally come and go. They meet other people, get married and have families of their own. But Susan is not seeing anyone else; Karen is her whole life. Susan does all the cleaning, cooking, household chores and asks nothing tangible in return. I could give Karen financial stability and security but that's not what she needs, and I don't want to be Karen's servant or her benefactor. Sometimes I feel protective towards her and, of course, I want her to be comfortable, but we're both grownups. Karen must be forced to choose between Susan and me and between the very different relationships we offer her.

Yet I dread Karen's final choice. I have no idea where I stand on her list of priorities. Where do I rank in relation to Susan, to Karen's work, to her business trips, her social life, her encounter sessions? Karen is willing to fly all the way to Mexico to interview a famous ballerina, just because she wants to publish the interview in a magazine. Would she fly as far to visit me?

The barriers that exist between Karen and me derive from her resistance to commitment. She won't admit that we are responsible for ourselves, that fate or time or the past or money doesn't control us. When I jokingly told her, "Beautiful women make their own rules," she shot back, "Men with money make their own rules!" Maybe. But we have both been making our own rules for a long time. If we lose by those rules, we have only ourselves to blame. Perhaps the commitment I demand frightens her because she's afraid that once I have it, I'll leave America again, depriving her even of the security she now has with Susan. She may be afraid that when I leave, my money will leave with me. Or she may fear that with me she will lose her independence. She has told me that she needs brief, perishable relationships because they give her the illusion that time is meaningless, that the end of one affair means the beginning of another, that the cycle of unpredictable events and wavering emotions makes her eternally available for a new adventure. For her, every free moment is a victory over the tedious roles of wife and mother that she might otherwise be playing. For me, every moment is a loss. Time has never seemed so precious. I feel powerless to make Karen understand, and I respond by making myself totally inaccessible to her.

I asked Anthony to lunch yesterday because he was my father's valet and because I think he might die soon. I want to learn more about my father from him.

During lunch Anthony told me why he was fired by my father after working for him for over twenty years. To prove his faith in American industry, my father insisted on shaving with an American-made steel blade for seven consecutive days. One of Anthony's duties was to prepare my father's soap and razor and for years he gave him a new blade once a week. However, my mother complained to Anthony that towards the end of the week my father was not shaven closely enough. After that Anthony began putting a new blade in the razor every two days without telling my father. One morning my father said, "The day before yesterday I shaved with a blade which had a slight defect at the end of its right edge. Still, it was a perfectly good blade and it should serve me until the end of the week. Where is it?" "I changed the blade, Mr. Whalen," replied Anthony. "What for?" asked my father. "I thought you might need a fresh one." "I do not," said my father. "Bring back the old blade."

When Anthony admitted he had thrown it away and had been changing blades every other day, my father turned to him and said calmly, "If that's what you think of American steel, Anthony, you needn't work for me any more, because I feel responsible for the quality of this steel. My secretary will prepare your pay check and after you've packed, the car will take you to the station." Then he returned to his shaving and didn't say another word to the man who for twenty years had served him like a faithful dog.

Anthony also told me that when my father learned

that General Motors had decided to manufacture a fiberglass car, the Corvette, he promptly called a Company board meeting. He stressed the point that the fate of millions of Americans depended on steel, not on fiberglass, and that his Company should cease its business with General Motors. Years later Studebaker announced production plans for its fiberglass Avanti. My father called the move blackmail, withdrew the Company's business from Studebaker and swore they would pay dearly for their desertion of the steel industry. According to Anthony, Studebaker soon faced serious financial difficulties. Finally, on the verge of bankruptcy, they ceased their entire car production in the United States.

"Have you decided what you're going to do with yourself, Jonathan?" Anthony asked me. "I gather you don't plan to go into business. You're still quite young, and it would be a pity, a real pity, to waste yourself doing nothing or doing the wrong things. How about sports? Your father was not a bad golfer and a good swimmer and he was self-taught. You can afford the best instructors, and in a short time you could develop real skill."

I told Karen today that she never completely expresses herself. The sexual aspect of life is missing from her interviews, her poems, even her fashion photographs. She agreed, but said she was afraid of exposing her real self. I suggested that she write in the third person and project her own sensibility onto her protagonists. It had never occurred to her. She said she was certain that people would criticize her writing according to their own standards, the way I criticize her relationship with Susan and with other men. She says I have given her reason to believe her fears are real.

During our lunch Anthony called my existence in New York just one more evasion. I resented that remark and changed the subject, chatting about my travels and how much I had learned, pretending to justify my past life. Then he said that I was lucky to have so much freedom, meaning money. I tried to explain that the freedom I have always desired has nothing to do with being able to travel or with surrendering responsibility; it means not being afraid, not disguising myself and not performing, not structuring my feelings to gain another's approval. I could see he wasn't interested. Again he seemed to be criticizing me, and that made me angry. When he told me how much I resembled my father, I was ready to walk out. Then it occurred to me that Anthony was not trying to tell me what was right; he was just a simple bitter man. I began talking about some of the women I had in Europe, asking him pointed questions about his own sex life, and telling him increasingly bizarre stories. We laughed together at first but as the episodes became more lewd and violent, he began to grow uncomfortable, and slumped down in his chair, exhausted by the possibility of such incredible adventures. I continued until I was sure he realized that my life was beyond his judgment.

Karen speaks fondly of Amsterdam. She says it is an ultimately civilized city where a foreigner doesn't have to make many adjustments, where everyone speaks English, where you can truly rest. Her response to Susan is much the same: Susan is familiar, undemanding, and with her Karen relaxes and acts spontaneously. They recognize each other's needs even when those needs come at inconvenient times. During our first week together, Karen asked if I thought loving was possible without complete emotional generosity. Her question sounded like an accusation. At that point in our relationship, her resistance to me was enormous and I knew that it would only increase the more I tried to counter it. She was afraid even then that I would insist she leave Susan. I have resisted making that demand, hoping that I could accept Susan's influence over Karen without jealousy.

At midnight I called the bookshop and asked them to send me twenty-five books of American poetry and twenty-five of translations of poetry, which they should select. An hour later they were delivered to my hotel room. This city is a dream: you can get anything at any hour of the day or night. Shortly afterwards, Karen called and said she wasn't well. Or perhaps she said she was depressed because Susan had just left for California. Instead of inviting Karen over or going to see her, I offered to read her one poem from each of the fifty volumes. She hung up before I reached volume two.

I know there are people who must be completely independent of others in order to feel free. For them, responding to someone else is like obeying a command. Any action that does not spring entirely from their own desires is false. I can understand this compulsion for detachment.

In a restaurant on First Avenue, I asked a girl at the bar if she wanted to go for a ride. We drove all over Manhattan with the latest pop songs blaring on the radio. I drove very fast and very badly, often not concentrating on the road. I think she was afraid. I began to contemplate making it with her, partly for the sake of a new experience, partly because I thought it might interest Karen if I told her about it. In a downtown bar I ordered a pitcher of Sangria and we sat very close to each other at a small table. The girl seemed very self-assured, and I sensed that every time she looked at me, she was assessing my body. I began to think of myself as an object of desire. I felt that she noticed everything about me, my gestures, the way my pants hugged my thighs, the way my hips moved. The more I concentrated on her image of me, the more I desired her. I tried to imagine myself in her place and wondered if she felt any apprehension at all. I asked her what it was like to be with a man she knew nothing about. She said that for a woman the strongest sexual stimulus is familiarity. The memory of past pleasures is the most potent of all aphrodisiacs. She said she could look at a man across a room and feel she already knew his body.

I told her I had a hotel suite. She laughed and asked to see it, so we went back there. Suddenly I knew I wanted to make love to her, yet I hesitated; she still seemed more at ease than I did. We talked about nothing much for half an hour. Then she said it was late and that she had to leave. I suggested she spend the night and that I would drive her home in the morning. She agreed.

I wanted to be honest and say: "Look, let's undress and make love," but instead I heard myself telling her, "Let's sleep in the same bed. It's large enough." Again she agreed readily; we undressed and got into bed. She moved easily into my arms and we caressed each other. At one point I was on top of her, stroking her hair and thinking, Soon, I'll put it in. But something, maybe the smell or texture of her hair, reminded me of Karen. Suddenly I no longer desired her. I felt sweaty and exhausted. Fucking her would merely have been an anecdote to tell Karen. I turned away from the girl and fell asleep.

In the morning, after the girl left, I called Karen. She

was caustic. She said that when people ask her what she does, she has to fight an impulse to stare at them and say, in an exaggerated Southern accent: "Actually, I suck cocks."

I had lunch with two of my former trustees. In the afternoon I signed papers and did some work with my lawyers. I thought about the girl I had picked up. She'd given me her phone number. I called and went over. Nothing unusual happened, but all the time I could feel myself slipping into another depression, and Somaphren didn't seem to make any difference. While she took a bath, I telephoned old friends, whose names and numbers I found in my old notebook. I couldn't reach any of them. They'd all moved while I'd been away. I went home and tried to go to sleep but couldn't. I called Karen; no answer. After a few drinks I called again. This time she answered and sounded drunk herself. I heard Susan's voice in the background. Karen giggled and chattered, and I imagined her and Susan making love. I started to masturbate but couldn't come, so I took another Somaphren, dozed off and dreamed my legs were being amputated. I woke up in the middle of the night wanting to call someone, anyone, the desk clerk, the telephone operator, the porter, but I resisted. Through it all an inquisitive voice kept saying: "So this is insanity. How interesting. What happens next?" The voice began to bore me and eventually I fell asleep. One dream repeated itself again and again: I was going down a flight of stairs in a subway station. The stair was lined on both sides with deformed women, their faces covered with sores. I had to run between the lines as the women reached for me. Suddenly the vision would change. One of the women was my mother. I saw her in her bedroom in Watch Hill, swallowing red pills, choking, trying to reach for her phone, staggering from her bed, with blood running down her leg. I woke up terrified, sweating heavily. I took some more pills, slept again fitfully and woke up at six feeling shaky.

There was hardly any death in my father's funeral. I never saw his corpse. There were speeches at the funeral home, banks of flowers, long lines of cars with their headlights on, crowds of people standing in the rain at the cemetery, black umbrellas, photographers, television cameras, and a police helicopter discreetly hovering above. That was all. I want to make up for it by imagining my mother's death.

My depressions are no longer such natural urges as sex, sleep and hunger. Now they are completely calculated. I could as easily have done something else yesterday afternoon, but I chose to enact a familiar ritual, to dull my mind and lose myself completely. I knew I was not genuinely upset the way I used to be. I was merely playing a familiar role, which I could abandon at any moment. Today at four in the afternoon I went to a liquor store and bought a fifth of Jack Daniel's. I went upstairs, poured myself a drink and put on a record. By six I had finished half the bottle and was thoroughly depressed, but comforted by the thought that I had selected my mood. I felt that at last I had total emotional control.

We met early in the evening, in a house near the beach. There were fifteen people, an up-tight group seated around a long table on straight-backed chairs. The most vocal were a black guy who said he hated me because he knew "who I was," a cold and slightly patronizing Jamaican girl from Stony Brook, and a woman history teacher from New York University, who seemed gentle and shy initially but who turned out to be the most belligerent person in the group. There were others who didn't interest me at all. Our group leader was assisted by a young nun from the Bronx whose obvious loneliness made everyone uneasy. In the beginning, I felt superior to the others, assuming that no one else could match my experiences abroad. How could these supermarket-psychotherapists understand what I went through in Rangoon and Munich?

After the first encounters two or three people admitted that my image was intimidating. A man from upstate said he envied my independence and wealth. Another said he would be frightened to have all my money. One girl said she would not like to go out with me: "What a sweat," she kept saying. Later someone called me "Superman," and accused me of being in the group because of guilt feelings about my money and family.

A girl who had just graduated from college broke

down and cried. Her boy friend was black and schizo-phrenic; she was torn between her own reality and her boy friend's. She said that she often had to listen to his secret whispers and enter his odious world. She sometimes slipped into his fantasies, she said, and each time anyone looked at her she believed that she was a white Negress.

The black guy spoke of feeling smothered because he was unable to express his emotions. He said his lack of education prevented him from articulating a cohesive story. He kept mumbling, "I don't make sense, I don't make sense," and when we tried to convince him that he did, he countered, "How do you know? You haven't lived my life. How do you know it makes sense?" I empathized with his despair, but despite my compassion, I remained detached from the group, aware that when people claim to know who I am, I can no longer act freely.

Someone said that the expenses for the group trip should be divided equally among us. He said many ghetto kids could have had a whole summer in the country for that kind of money. The black man quickly agreed. The tall blonde girl blew up at him; she protested that she wasn't concerned with the money; she couldn't care less about the black, red, yellow or white children. She was here not to solve societal problems of underprivileged races, but wanted us to get back to gut level. She accused him of cutting down white people simply because they weren't black, instead of admitting to the real sources of his anger. I felt threatened by her outburst. She had supported me before and I had responded warmly, but now I felt betrayed. Later when I told her about it, she said that I probably expected betrayal from everyone, especially from women, whom I clearly do not understand. I said that I was surprised to hear her speak of understanding since it takes years to develop and occurs only when people feel free to expose themselves to one another. To speak of understanding before this point is a mockery.

I was nervous all day long, and could think of nothing but the next encounter meeting. I canceled a morning appointment with my brokers and lay in bed, rehearsing what I would say. But by nighttime I was already in the lodge in Vermont and the counselor was introducing me as "the new protagonist." I felt shaky and admitted it to the group. When someone asked me to walk across the room, my knees were painfully stiff, and I decided that I should present at least two of my selves in my encounter. I designated one man as my vulnerable self, another as the invulnerable one. One girl as my mother, another as a nanny.

The first scene took place in my bedroom at home. In

one area we established the little blue dresser in which I had kept my toys and books, and in another my small rocking chair. A black girl played my nanny. She touched my hair, combing and playing with it, then she pretended to cut it; she rambled on: "This is such a bother, when I have so much to do. This house is a circus." I was laughing, but when she said, "Your father will be home soon," I suddenly became upset. It must have been noticeable, because someone in the group turned off the lights. But even with the protection of darkness I felt I must not give in to my emotions. I maintained my self-control and soon I was at ease.

Then we enacted the news of my father's death. I remembered walking out of our summer house and hearing the phone ring. Then my nanny came out and said somberly, "Jonathan, your father is on his way to heaven." I ran to my father's room and rocked in his chair, reading my little red leather Bible with "Jonathan" on its cover in gold letters. In the encounter I made the girl say: "Looks like your father is dying." I don't know why I changed the words.

As a boy I got the idea that death was an animal which lay curled inside waiting to swallow us. Ever since then, when I sense the creature lying inside me, I feel as if I were a boy again, sitting in that rocking chair.

We moved on to a dialogue with my mother. I remember spilling orange juice on the morning she was to go to the hospital for a checkup. It upset her. Later, when she returned from the hospital, she said, "I tried to be a good mother, Jonathan, but the only thing you will remember about me is that I got angry with you for spilling orange juice." As I acted out my mother's role, I realized for the first time the agony she must have experienced when she began to suspect she was disturbed. She would never know how her child would turn out. She would never see me as a man, but always as a boy, as I was the year I went away.

Now the girl who played my mother sat in a chair quite far from me. I wanted to ask her about the really important moments she had shared with my father. I began to wonder if I was taking up too much of everyone else's time.

Then a voice suddenly shouted, "You're fucking up our session, Jonathan." The history teacher said she had never before met anyone as controlled as I was. Only someone of my background, she said, could act out a tragedy one minute and a burlesque the next. She said that I would never really let go, that I would always resist my impulses and remain detached.

The girl from Stony Brook said that in this country we don't think enough of sex to believe that anyone could restrict his obsessions to it. In America, a man who is overtly preoccupied with sex is automatically considered a pervert, an alcoholic, an addict, a criminal, an all-around deviate. We expect to find all the social ills in his mind and body, and because we expect to find them, we do.

Last summer, she said, there was a voyeur in her neighborhood who pretended to be a police photographer. The voyeur walked around taking pictures of trees and flowers while secretly peeping through half-opened curtains of bedrooms and bathrooms. Whenever he was questioned about his curious behavior, he said he was a detective assigned to drug control. Ironically, about the same time the police discovered several makeshift hothouses for marijuana plants in her community. One couple had grown several hundred plants in their bedroom closet, using ultraviolet lamps, heaters and sheets of aluminum simulating sunlight. Many arrests followed, and the neighbors stopped mistrusting the voyeur. But the police became aware of the man and started following him. One day when he was doing nothing out of the ordinary, he was arrested on a charge of obscene behavior. They beat him up and broke his cameras. After that he began drinking. He was picked up again, this time for disturbing the peace. When he returned, he no longer pretended to be a policeman. Instead, he started dressing like Superman, wearing a cape and boots and skintight suit with an "S" pierced by flashing thunderbolts embroidered on the chest, like a huge dollar sign. He was seen leaping from roof to roof.

Then he was arrested once more, this time for trespassing and intimidating children. When he came back from jail, he was very thin and did not wear his outfit any more. Soon he disappeared. A few days later his building superintendent went to inspect the man's one-room apartment. When the refrigerator door wouldn't open easily, he pulled harder, but the door still wouldn't move. He went to get help and when they finally forced open the refrigerator, they found Superman inside wearing his costume. Apparently he had swallowed a bottle of sleeping pills and then decided to preserve himself.

There was a fat, ugly girl in the group who I assumed disliked me, but during one of the sessions she told me what bad vibrations she picked up from me. With tears in her eyes, she said she felt I had been terribly hurt and that

I brought out her maternal instincts. I was embarrassed and I put my hands over my face. For a moment I longed for this girl or any other woman there to take me in her arms. I told the girl that I was moved by what she said, and that if she really knew me she wouldn't feel that way. For the rest of the day I couldn't push aside the realization that in all my life I had been held only by Mademoiselle Irène, my nanny, and the whores I paid to make love to me. I wished that I could be with Mademoiselle Irène, an old woman now, and ask her not to say anything but simply to hold me.

Here we are, I thought, a bunch of grown-up kids locked in an empty room playing naïve games with each other. No one understands anybody else. We are wandering around in dark caves, holding our little private candles, hoping for some great illumination. I don't like to think I'm as confused or simple-minded as the others, but if I really am more complex, more experienced than they are, why should I want them to understand me?

I thought of Karen and how skeptical she is about the encounter group and why she refuses to come now that she knows I will be there. She finds the whole idea of it false. In a sense I do too.

I miss Karen. I see her as someone who has been hurt in exactly the same way I have been hurt, but if I try to reach her on that level, she may think that I'm attempting to analyze her in order to smash her defenses. She would be wrong: I'm not playing analyst. Her distrust of others is much stronger than mine and I know how difficult it is to penetrate because I know the measure of my own distrust.

Only two days ago we arrived here, perfect strangers to each other. In the adjoining parking lot we neatly parked our respective air-conditioned Furies, Tempests, Rebels, Swingers and Demons. Now, two days later, we are still strangers, anxious to return to our individual existence, and all the tears and hugs and screams and anger seem vacuous and unreal. This concept of instant intimacy annoys me more than anything else about the encounter group. It breaks down resistances and makes people feel good by allowing them to think that they are really getting to know one another. Yet in the end nothing has happened; we know no more about ourselves and the others than we would after a cocktail party.

Yesterday I met Keith, whom I had not seen since we both were in Katmandu. He seemed much more serious than I had remembered him. For some reason he was obsessed with different modes of reproduction. He said that mankind has always been mystified by birth and has offered various theories of its origin. Aristotle, for instance, thought eels were born spontaneously out of decayed sun-heated sea weeds, from the hot guts of the earth. We think we are the most complex of nature's creations, Keith said, but there are many more interesting species. He explained that there are creatures, like the jellyfish, which exist in two completely different forms. One generation reproduces by sexual fertilization but its offspring is asexual and through simple budding produces a generation which again reproduces sexually.

Keith thought that I had changed, that I seemed listless and disinterested in everything. He said his own life had changed radically when he became involved with nature, and he recommended several books to me. But I'm skeptical about that kind of zeal, whether it's political, religious, mystical or whatever. The last time I saw him he was involved with world revolution, and before that with semantics. Like most people, Keith is simply searching for an activity to label his existence. He said it was impossible to explain his new involvement with nature because our language has lost its ability to convey the spontaneous. This bothered me because he was plainly placing me among those hopelessly precise types whom I despise as much as he does. I believe that I have a strong intuition and am not by any means a literalist. Still, Keith was perfectly right to recognize how poorly we communicate. No one can help me find answers, least of all someone who claims he's found a solution to life.

Susan tends to divide people into two groups: those who have had personal catastrophes, and those who haven't. She was interested when she learned that I had been through an unbroken chain of disasters: The death of my parents. Drug addiction. Illness. But she doesn't think I've achieved a greater degree of self-awareness than people who have led uneventful lives. I once told her that I can't say anything about myself without at some point contradicting my own statement while believing both statements to be equally true. She says I don't know how to define myself, that I am unable to make such a simple assertion as: "I always do this or that," or "I am the sort of person who generally does this or that." Susan was frank enough to tell me what Karen's friends think of me. I hadn't suspected that they talked about me so much. I was visibly upset by what she said, so she shifted the conversation and began to talk about herself. "Most people," she said, "are probably looking for lovers with whom they can share basic interests. In my case, I'm looking for someone who can make me feel pain and fear, who can expose my real hang-ups."

Today, when the group discussed prejudice, everyone was serious and apologetic. Finally I said, "Look, we're all very concerned about prejudice and we should be, but after all, there are only three black people in the group, while there are several others here who are also victims of prejudice. And we aren't talking about their problems at all." At once attention centered completely on me. Whom did I mean? Were the men who take care of my money prejudiced against me? When had anyone ever denied me anything? Then someone asked why all the talk was directed at me. One woman suggested it was because I was articulate and had been overseas and was rich. I was clearly discriminated against because of my privileged status. Another suggested that it was because in the world of the homely, I was still handsome. Then they all began to analyze me. One person said I was obviously very strong, another that I was just as obviously sensitive, and another that I was "masculine but soft." The black guy said that I frightened him although he didn't know why. I asked them to stop giving me their flack and to get down to real feelings.

During this discussion Anita, who had slept with me the night before, was brooding silently. When someone asked her about our relationship, she replied: "I wish I knew; maybe he'll tell me sometime." Then she became very angry, and shouted at me: "How can you be so serious about this group and still play all those little games which cast us in roles you've devised?" I shouted back that she was the one who allowed me to invent those roles.

The black guy said that even though I frightened him he wanted to protect me. "All that money," he said, pointing at me, "running around in the person of one unhappy man." Everybody laughed. Then he said Anita was hung up on me, and that several of the other girls in the group were too. All this attention flatters me but at the same time I know it's completely superficial. These people see exactly what they want to see, and what they want to see is a spoiled rich boy, dissatisfied with life.

Karen says that I will continue to be an important but not essential part of her life. By letting many men define her, she will avoid smothering and driving any one of us away. Her demand for attention is so great that no one man can possibly fulfill it. She feels that any man who appreciates the extent of her need will be overwhelmed. According to Susan, Karen always chooses men with the power to destroy her; unless she feels threatened, she becomes so bored that she leaves. She vacillates between seeing herself as the predator and as the prey.

Karen is certain that her fantasies about sodomy with old men would be just as terrifying to me as her fantasies of marrying me, having my child, serving tea in the late afternoon. She pointed out that my ego is as fragile as hers: after each date both of us are sure we will never meet again. She also admitted that she is beginning to visualize the end of her relationship with Susan. "I still need her reassurance," Karen said, "but not as much as before. I have more self-confidence now. I can imagine you and me ending up together."

I had the good fortune to meet your mother about two years after your father's death. Shortly before we met, several of my articles on ancient cultures had been published in popular magazines and I was beginning to earn a reputation as an archeologist. Through my work I had met a Persian antique dealer, who sold your mother a large collection of art objects. That spring your mother invited him to stay with her in Pittsburgh for a week, and since he knew very little English, he asked me to come along to translate. About two weeks after our visit, your mother invited me to dine with her, and after dinner she asked me to translate the catalogue that accompanied her newly acquired objects. She offered to pay me, but I refused. On the following day I sent her some of the books I'd written and underlined passages I thought might interest her.

I found your mother very attractive, Mr. Whalen. You might ask if I would have found her as attractive if she had been an ordinary office girl. But you see, she was not an ordinary office girl. She was Mrs. Katherine Whalen, widow of Horace Whalen. Just as an office girl is inseparable from her dreary job, your mother was inseparable from the elegant world through which she moved.

After a few more translating assignments, I invited your mother to dinner out of town. We talked about everything: art galleries, books, the Babylonians, her collection of miniatures, my projects, her marriage.

That's how it began. From then on I saw her twice, perhaps three times, a week. We went to the movies— before she met me she had never been to a drive-in—to the theater, museums, lectures, art shows. We met only when she was at her best, but regardless of whether it was at your mother's invitation or mine, I always paid the check. For quite some time there was no physical intimacy between us; we merely enjoyed each other's company.

You must remember that I am not a rich man, Mr. Whalen. My father was an insurance broker who left no estate. I support my mother in Florida. When I met Mrs. Whalen I had about seventy-five thousand dollars invested in various stocks, and about fifteen thousand in a savings account. In fifteen years that's all I had managed to save from the royalties on my books. Until I met your mother I had always lived a carefully planned life. But whenever she and I went out for the evening I ended up spending more in one night then I normally spent in a month.

Finally I was forced to choose which was more important: financial security or the company of a woman unlike anyone I had ever known or would ever meet again. I chose your mother.

When we became lovers, she decided that we should be very discreet. She did not plan to marry again. She didn't want to cause gossip which would hurt you and embarrass the Company.

To make our relationship less apparent, your mother would invite one of her older lady friends to go with us whenever we visited places where she was well known.

Because of our mutual interest in antiquity, we decided we would visit sites neither of us had ever seen. At that time your mother didn't suffer from the malaise that later affected her. She loved to travel, enjoyed good food and was a marvelous companion.

She insisted on paying for our trips, because she liked to stay in the best hotels. She always requested the largest suites, and the hotel management was asked to put additional staff at her disposal. Your mother never carried cash. The wages and the standard service charge for all these people were included in the hotel bill, which was sent directly to your mother's bank.

Not that your mother didn't pay attention to her money. She was quite concerned with the stock market. I recall that once when we were in Venice she heard from her bank that the market was very bearish and that she had lost money. During lunch on the terrace overlooking the Grand Canal I inquired about news from home. She said that the recession had gotten worse; "nasty," she called it. She said that on the previous day she had lost close to sixty-two million dollars. "On paper, of course!" She laughed. In the afternoon she asked for the latest American newspapers; when one of the hotel managers delivered them, she joked that *Pravda* was probably more accurate than the *Wall Street Journal* at predicting what would happen on the Street. Immediately the hotel manager offered to bring your mother the latest edition of *Pravda*.

"Where can you get it in Venice?" she asked him. "I receive it by mail at home, madam. I subscribe to it," he said. "But I don't know Russian," she said. "If you wish, I could translate any articles that particularly interest you," he volunteered. Your mother was surprised and asked him why he read *Pravda*. "I am a Communist," he answered. "I studied the history of capitalism in the Soviet Union." Your mother was taken aback—the hotel was one of her favorites—nevertheless, she agreed, and he brought several articles, which she said gave an even vaguer explanation of the market's downfall than the New York *Times*.

As I said, during our trips your mother never carried cash, so I took care of the tips when we left each place. Eventually I began carrying an attaché case filled with ones, fives and tens, ready for tipping.

As I recall, I gave about ten dollars to each hall porter, ten to the headwaiter, five to the sommelier, twenty-five to the ship steward and purser, five to the bell captain, five to each of the maids and valets, forty to each archeological guide, one hundred to hotel managers, twenty-five to desk clerks in charge of theater tickets; seamstresses got forty, hotel telephone operators, secretaries, chauffeurs, masseuses, beauticians, and hairdressers got twenty-five each. In addition there were restaurants and bars, taxis, garages, ships and trains, airports, country inns, health spas. Naturally people, even the donkey and mule drivers, expected to be tipped; and because of how and where we traveled I had to buy appropriate clothes and luggage continually. By the end of the second year of our relationship, I had only two thousand dollars left and was nowhere near finishing my book about ancient Thera.

I never discussed any of this with your mother. How could I? To explain that I had run out of money tipping waiters would be to admit my total dependence on her. Instead, I wrote her that it was imperative that I finish my book quickly and that I wouldn't be able to see her until it was completed. Within a week she had left the country on a boat trip. I never saw her again.

When I was six years old, my father used to show me the countryside outside of Pittsburgh. Every day I was allowed to sit next to him and work the gearshift of the car, while he worked the clutch. One afternoon we saw two men in hunter's caps and leather jackets running along the highway with rifles. When we heard shots, my father stopped the car. Soon the hunters appeared dragging a dead deer. The sight of the animal and its blood on the highway fascinated me. I thought it would be wonderful to hunt down an animal.

I still dreamed of the chase when I went to Africa years later. Instead, I found myself standing at a muddy water hole in the midst of the Kenya bush, sharing a pair of binoculars with a paunchy Prussian businessman, his albino Frau, and their Americanized daughter. I remember leaning out the open roof of their air-conditioned Safari Mercedes, watching a pair of baboons mate behind a tree.

Keith called to tell me his violent rages are beginning to destroy his relationship with Patricia. He is going back into therapy.

An hour later Karen called. "I love to have my period," she said, "to feel the warm steady pull of blood. I hate the way the pills reduce my flow. I'm going to stop taking them." She had just returned from a meeting of the local New Woman Society, at which they had decided that deodorants are to sex what censorship is to free expression; they suppress the real taste and smell of a body. Karen was furious that anyone could prefer the synthetic scents of raspberry, jasmine, orange blossom and champagne to the pungency of the glands. "They force us to take the pill," Karen said, "they force us to shave our hair, they want to penetrate our brains as well as our vaginas." She did not say who "they" were, and I didn't ask.

It's a strange week, and I have been hibernating. One day I lie on the hotel roof garden in my swimming trunks beneath a bright-blue sky. The next day I walk home through cold, grey streets lined with battered garbage cans, with the wind wrapping old papers around my ankles.

This morning I bought several newspapers and magazines devoted entirely to sex. One of them featured a well-written editorial supporting the state's liberal candidate and vigorously protesting American genocide in Vietnam. In the adjoining columns were photographs of naked people fornicating and doing fellatio. Captions headlined cunt tricks and screwing stratagems and claimed that a big hard cock is not enough for the new superclit female who demands more from her superstud partner than dildos or sperm.

Reading these newspapers made me aware of how long I've been gone and how far away I've been.

I'm getting accustomed to automotive life. On the Manhattan expressway near my building, a black man was struck by a car during the evening rush hour. The unending stream of automobiles ran over him again and again in the rapid traffic. Finally the police, acting upon a single complaint, retrieved the battered mass of flesh.

In the Bronx a state trooper who was called to the scene of a multicar collision in a heavily wooded area failed to notice one of the cars, which had been thrown through the guardrail. The car was eventually found in a ravine. Several hundred yards from the car they found the passengers, who had apparently lived long enough to crawl away in an effort to reach the turnpike. I hate to think what would have happened if they had.

Karen told me that one of the best copy writers she knew had killed himself. He was a P.O.W., released by Hanoi, who had just recently appeared before some sort of Congressional investigating committee. In the P.O.W. camp he had allegedly been given the job of dividing the incoming prisoners into categories, deciding which ones were fit for work and which weren't. He was accused of favoring those P.O.W.'s whose political thinking had, so to speak, been influenced by the Communists. The committee wanted to know why the only survivors of the camp were those prisoners who had been successfully indoctrinated against American defense policies. He was accused of betraying all the loyal P.O.W.'s to the enemy.

He tried to defend himself by saying that the P.O.W.'s most determined to survive were men who loved something more tangible than the Department of Defense. Needless to say, the committee did not accept his interpretation.

Karen was surprised by all the articles on masturbation in "liberated" newspapers and magazines, complete with diagrams and detailed instructions. "I thought masturbation was instinctive," she said. "I never imagined people needed to be taught." She told me that when she was about six she had felt a pleasant physical sensation as she was clinging to one of the metal poles supporting a slide. Years later, while she was lying on the porch hammock, she discovered she could re-create the sensation by rubbing her body against the stiff fabric of the swinging hammock. She never had any difficulty masturbating. Gradually, however, she began to feel guilty about it. She also admitted that in bed she can never tell a man what she really wants. "I've been conditioned," she said, "to please men and to take my pleasure only from pleasing them; I don't know what I want. When a man does ask me how he can make it good for me—and that doesn't happen much—I can't tell him what I want. I've learned to fake coming, but I despise those men who believe my act."

Karen said that she felt compelled to do it their way in exchange for the companionship and approval she needed from them. She dreaded being in bed with these men because she was repulsed by her own willingness to compromise. But even more she dreaded the thought of sex with men with whom she could honestly abandon herself. She was afraid that once they saw what she really was, they would leave her.

A married couple she knew called Karen and asked her to go to a movie with them. Afterwards, they all went back to her apartment. In the kitchen the wife confided to Karen that her marriage was threatened because her husband had begun sleeping with other women without her consent or participation.

After they all had smoked some grass, the couple asked Karen if they could make love in her bedroom. Karen offered to go shopping. "Stay," they said. "Why don't you join us?" She did. In the beginning they all admitted their embarrassment. Karen and the woman discussed their mutual shyness and their fears of inadequacy. All three found it easy to fondle breasts but were reticent about going down on each other. So the evening went by: they made love and discussed their reactions. Karen told me how arousing it had been to fantasize making love to them and then actually do it. She claimed that during this experience she was more excited and uninhibited than ever before.

Karen told me about an old woman who was the last surviving inhabitant of one of the Hermit Islands. She was the only one left who could speak her tribe's language, but the anthropologists didn't realize it and never bothered to learn it from her. When the old woman died, the language died with her.

In the toilet of a downtown restaurant, I read the graffiti: "Do you realize that one out of every four Americans is unbalanced? Think of your three closest

friends. If they seem normal, then you are the one."
Three closest friends! I have one close friend, a woman
whom I love, and I am unable to tell her what I feel.

Karen is bitter. She remembered that before I went
abroad I told her I end relationships once I get bored.
It frightened her to think she might be too easily known to
keep me interested or that her full complexity might
elude me. She despises the ways in which most people gain
access to each other. They relate only through tedious
questions and impersonal physical facts. She said she
would like to go abroad and wear silk pajamas and
wander the earth, sleeping with everyone she desires,
making love in threesomes and foursomes, trying everything.

Whalen ordered a drink. Two men standing next to him glanced at him and continued talking. Fragments of their conversation reached him above the din of the jukebox and television set. The bartender rinsed a glass, filled it with liquor and pushed it towards Whalen.

Whalen leaned back and looked along the bar. A black girl sat on one of the tall stools, her right elbow resting against the bar, one leg dangling off the stool. She was alone. He finished his drink, ordered another and walked over to her.

"I'm Jonathan—I hope you don't mind my squeezing in here?" he said and laid his hand beside hers on the counter.

"I don't mind," she answered.

"I wondered if you might like to go somewhere else. We could drive out of town."

"What for?" she asked.

"There's a house I want to see. No one lives in it. About an hour out of town—it's a nice drive." The girl listened, sipping her drink.

"What I want to know is why should I go for a ride to some Godforsaken barn with some white dude I don't know and don't want to know?"

"Well, it's quite a place. Lots of rooms, old furniture, paintings. It has a swimming pool, its own park and a telescope."

"Why do you want me to go with you?" She played

with her empty glass. "Are you going to rip off something?"

"No," said Whalen. "I used to live there. It's been empty for years now. I feel like walking with you through those rooms and looking through the drawers."

"In the middle of the night, here in Shitsburgh, you feel like visiting your old house with me?" She laughed.

Whalen smiled. "My mother used to call this town the same thing."

By coincidence, just before my departure for Pittsburgh, a man telephoned me and introduced himself as a collector of rare papers and letters. He said that he had come upon a number of my father's letters to my mother. I didn't believe him, but asked him to bring the letters to my hotel so I could decide whether or not I wanted to buy them. The envelopes were postmarked from various parts of the country and written on stationery from many hotels and clubs. The letters must have been sent during his business trips.

I asked the man how he had acquired the letters. He said many valuable things had been scattered throughout my mother's houses and that some of the really interesting memorabilia had probably been stolen after my mother's death, before the houses were sealed.

When he left, I tried to read the letters, but they were all handwritten and I couldn't decipher my father's scrawl.

"This country's culture is antiseptic. No one wants to talk about disease and lameness. People are terrified of malformation. No big corporation would promote a hunchback. Our foundations hesitate to invite a prominent scientist if he's physically grotesque. Mind you, it's not because those businesses or foundations have anticripple policies. It's just that in this country a deformed man makes his audience apprehensive. Can you imagine a dwarf running for the Senate? People prefer to avoid confronting deformity and when they do it's only for kicks. A midget, for instance, because he combines the experience of a grownup with the appearance of a child, excites the sexually insecure. In America you've got to be as straight as a highway."

"When I saw them in Africa, I thought these birds were the greatest fliers of all. Hardly beating their wings, they fly for hours, swooping upwards on air currents with no sign of physical effort. But when they land, they pitch forward on their stubby legs without stopping. They skid along on their bellies, their necks straining to absorb the shock of the landing. Their beaks dig into the sand and they collide with anything in their path. Quite often they break their wings or beaks or spines and remain for the rest of their lives in the scrubby thickets not far from where they crash. The crippled birds sit there blind, paralyzed or in shock, and struggle slowly back and forth to their nests. Some hop on one leg, some drag their crippled wings behind them like broken umbrellas. I wonder whether they ever envy their brothers soaring in the air or if they're glad to be grounded and past their trial."

"Another time I saw two squid copulate. They approach each other very slowly, keeping their heads stiff and their tentacles floating about them. First the female lowers herself onto the sea bed and spreads her swaying arms. Then the male descends like a parachute, fits his arms into hers, and both of them rock back and forth. When the male senses the time is right, he puts the tentacle that's full of sperm into the female's cavity. But that entry is through her breathing funnel, and unless she's really in heat, she feels choked and tries to break away. In the course of the struggle she often tears off the arm caught in her. The crippled squid swims away, while his severed tentacle stays alive inside the female. When she finally slackens, the arm is released and swims away."

"It's still alive?"

"Yes. For a long time biologists didn't know that the things they call sea serpents are really the squid's copulatory tentacles."

"Didn't they notice that some male squid had arms missing?"

"No. After the copulatory tentacle—"

"That name breaks me up."

"After the arm is severed, the squid grows a new one. That's why those sea serpents were so puzzling. They didn't copulate with each other and no one could figure out what sex they were or how they were born."

"What sex were they?"

"Neuter. For the squid, the sea serpent is sex itself!"

The walls were faded, almost pastel. Some of them were painted with delicate designs while others were hung with tapestries, portraits or dim, unsigned landscapes. The carpets were dusty, and the parquet floor was scratched. Whalen lifted the dust sheets to look at the delicate chairs, with legs and arms intricately carved. Small tables were still placed strategically near window nooks and love seats to hold teacups and sherry glasses. The furniture was waiting to be used again, refusing to lose its purpose along with its polish.

His mother's bathroom door was half open. In the medicine cabinet he could see an infinity of drug samples, many still in the manufacturer's packages, accompanied by printed inserts indicating dosage and warnings. He glanced through the inserts: "to alleviate anxiety and tension," "reversal of psychotic behavior patterns," "for management of overt hostility associated with chronic schizophrenia due to organic brain disease," "recommended for patients under close supervision," "to alleviate severe apathy, agitation, psychomotor retardation," "overdosage might produce stupor, coma, shock, respiratory depression and death."

She sat up, stuffed a pillow behind her back and lit a cigarette. After a moment she got up, walked slowly towards the door and snapped off the overhead light. Then she turned and went to the walk-in closet. She opened the door and stepped inside, turning on the closet light. She began taking off her clothes, carefully hanging them on hangers. She turned to face him and eased her stockings down. Then her hands moved behind her back to unhook her bra. She hung it on the doorknob and stepped out of her underpants. In the dim light he saw her tongue touch her lips, making them glisten. Without a word she reached down, took his hand, and raised it to her nipples, then pushed it lower. She pressed her hand against her stomach, breathed in, then exhaled. Her flesh was warm and dry, without a trace of dampness. She threw back her head and sat down, waiting.

She lifted herself, hesitated, then slowly came closer to him. When she turned her face away, he kissed her neck, slid down on the bed and kissed the back of her thigh. His mouth was dry and he felt only her skin's sandy surface. His pulse began to race. Once when he was skin-diving, he had surprised a deep-water snake lying coiled in thick coral. The snake followed him, its lidless eyes open, spiraling effortlessly through the water. He remembered how he had tired quickly, slowing down, feeling conquered. He had hated the creature with its one light lung in which it seemed to store more air than he carried in two heavy tanks. He envied the snake's ability to control its heartbeat, to slow its pace even as it attacked.

Both bed lamps were on but she was asleep. He could see her uneven make-up cracked by tiny wrinkles under her eyes, and matted with perspiration at the base of her nose. He was the audience, and she was on stage. He approached the bed and stood quietly beside it. Her head lay on the pillow exactly at the level of his knees. He rested his hand on the blanket and it occurred to him that she was only pretending to be asleep, anticipating his wanting to touch her. He drew his hand back and returned to his chair. From there he continued to watch her.

Whalen opened the portfolio and immediately recognized his father's stationery: "Dear Jonathan, On Friday, July 27th, I sent back to the Summer Camp a form indicating that you would be coming home by train, and enclosed our check for fifty-three dollars and sixty-one cents. The camp will purchase your train ticket and give you fifteen dollars traveling money to cover meals and other incidentals. We are getting you a parlor-car seat in the pullman so that you will be comfortable. They will serve you lunch and dinner in the same car, so that you only have to ask the porter to tell you when to get off. You can give him a fifty-cent tip for the trip to Pittsburgh, and the same to the waiter. Your schedule is as follows: Saturday, August 18th, the camp closes at 10 A.M. The people at the camp will put you on the train at Plymouth, Indiana. Your train's name is The Fort Pitt. It leaves at 10:56 A.M. and arrives in Pittsburgh at 7:45 P.M. You can tell the porter I will be on hand to meet you. I'm sure he will know who I am. Enjoy the rest of your stay at the camp and come back full of vim and vigor. Have a good trip. Cordially, Your father."

He picked up another letter neatly typed on the Company stationery. "My dear Son, I have received two letters from you; they give me much pleasure because, as you know, I miss you very much and am looking forward to being with you in another eight or nine days. Your mother and I talk about you every day. Since she is more

127

in touch with your school than I am, she knows how well you are getting along there, which of course I expected. I'm glad the weather is fine where you are, because it's anything but fine here. Today it's raining and very disagreeable. I assume you are playing tennis and swimming every day, which is good for your health. Keep up the good work and take care of yourself. We look forward to seeing you soon. With lots of love, Father." On the letter's bottom-left corner, there were the traces of an additional sentence which had been erased: "Dictated but not read."

The next letter, from the Dean of the College, had been written just before Whalen went abroad. "The committee has reviewed your record for the spring semester. As you know, you failed English, Political Science, History and Anthropology. You also failed to raise your Grade Point Index to the minimum requirement. As your record to date gives no substantive proof that you are capable of academic discipline and achievement, it is the committee's recommendation that you be dismissed from the College. After due consideration, I have accepted their recommendation, and have instructed the registrar that you shall not be permitted to enroll for the coming semester. I regret the necessity of this action and wish you every success in the future."

Whalen was amused to find a letter from the office of the mayor addressed to "Jonathan James Whalen, Esq." "Dear Jonathan, No words of mine can ease your sorrow at the loss of your father, but I want you to know my thoughts are with you. I remember your father in my prayers. There is little else we mortals can do. My warmest personal regards. John Lee Overholt, Mayor."

In the same stack, he found a handwritten letter to his father from the White House. "My Dearest Friend, At all times in the campaign one of my great comforts has been the knowledge that we would never lack the needed funds to bring the message of our Crusade to all our fellow Americans. I cannot begin to thank you for the way in which you performed a vital and difficult task, but I wish to assure you of my deep gratitude. You have done a magnificent job, both as a friend and as a Republican. As we begin the crucial task of putting campaign pledges into effect for the benefit of our country, I anticipate your advice and your support. With all best wishes to you, Katherine and Jonathan—" It was signed by the President.

He picked up a folder of newspaper clippings and leafed through it: HORACE SUMNER WHALEN DIES DROWNING, INDUSTRY EMPIRE-BUILDER THE SEA'S VICTIM, CIVIC LEADERS MOURN WHALEN. HORACE SUMNER WHALEN LEADER OF AMERICAN INDUSTRY DIES IN HEAVY SEAS OFF HIS RHODE ISLAND HOME.

Other clippings gave fragments of his father's biography: "Born in Colorado, never completed his elementary education." "He was forced at the age of thirteen to leave school to find work after the death of his father.

129

Sumner Whalen got his first job as an office boy with an aluminum company at four dollars and eighty-five cents a week. Advancing rapidly to positions of increasing responsibility, Mr. Whalen became a plant manager at the age of twenty-three. Two years later he founded his own company, which was successful from the start. It soon became obvious that Whalen's Company would undergo a major expansion." "The sudden death of Horace Sumner Whalen writes the final chapter in the saga of the rise of American heavy industry, and the determined individualists who led it. Andrew Carnegie, Henry Clay Frick, Charlie Schwab, B. F. Jones, Henry Phipps, Jr., and Horace Whalen are the heroes of that story. They were tough men, engaged in a tough business. And they helped to make this nation tough." "Horace Sumner Whalen many years ago told reporters that he started every day with the same prayer, read Dickens for inspiration and listened to Bach's Toccata and Fugue in D minor at least once a day."

Whalen picked up the program of the Annual Dinner of the Institute of American Heavy Industry given in his father's honor. Its cover was made of thick aluminum foil; in the center was a raised plate medallion engraved with the Institute's symbol, the running bull, and credo, "A Great and Growing Country." The program listed an address by the Institute's President and a speech, "SEATO —Power for Peace," by the USA Supreme Allied Commander Southeast Asia. The menu consisted of bisque de langouste with sherry, golden croutons, filet of boeuf à la mode, golden fleurons, salad, frozen soufflé Alaska, cherries jubilee flambée, petits fours and demitasse. Whalen tried to picture his father unfolding his napkin, appreciating the meal and applauding politely after the speeches.

In a separate album he found clippings about the death of his mother. They were newer, mounted between sheets of transparent plastic. "Mrs. Katherine Furston Peck Whalen, widow of Horace Sumner Whalen and one of America's richest women, died last night at her winter home in Palm Springs. Mrs. Whalen bore the mantle of grande dame of American industry with grace and ease. She presided over a forty-room mansion in Pittsburgh, and after the death of Horace Whalen continued to maintain the family's homes in Watch Hill, Palm Springs, and their yacht on the Côte d'Azur. Her jewelry alone was estimated to be worth—" Whalen glanced at numerous other clippings. "She was attending school in," "they were married," "when Horace Sumner Whalen died, Mrs. Whalen inherited over a quarter of a billion dollars in municipal bonds alone," "Mrs. Whalen was grief-stricken for years after her husband's death despite the consolation of her youth and her son," "Following the example of her late husband Mrs. Whalen left her entire estate in trust to her only son. The trust for Jonathan James Whalen, one of the largest in this country, has been placed in the hands of National Midland—," "Jonathan Whalen has been living abroad, where he combines study with travel."

Another folder contained sheets of unused postage stamps bearing his father's portrait. A letter signed by the Postmaster General was attached to one of the sheets: "We are happy to present you with the first official sheet of this new stamp which commemorates your husband's pioneering role in American industry. Additional sheets will be available to the members of your family and to the directors and officers of your Company and others whom you designate."

Whalen couldn't remember ever having mailed or received a letter with this stamp. Perhaps no one had ever thought to tell him when it was issued. There were so many other stamps bearing portraits of great men. He wondered whether his father would have been upset at being selected for a stamp that could be used only on surface postcards.

The memories triggered no emotion. He recalled coming home from camp, seeing the long black car waiting for him at the station. He remembered sitting next to the chauffeur and reading the passing signs— Sweetheart Brands, Forge and Pipe Works, Half Moon Island, Moon Run Road, Moontour Run—thinking how strange the familiar names sounded. He could almost hear his father explaining to him that the Peter Tarr blast furnace produced cannon balls used by Oliver Hazard Perry in the War of 1812, and that Horace Sumner Whalen was now sole owner of all the land surrounding the furnace for miles and miles. Years later, one of his mother's drunken guests drove the car into the swimming pool.

Deeper in the drawer he found a yearbook from the Samuel Tuke Upper School for Girls. He turned the pages until he came to his mother's photograph. She looked girlish and frail. Her fingers seemed unnaturally long.

The yearbook noted that she was a Merit Finalist, won

first prize in the Alpha Omega poetry contest, and was a member of Cum Laude, Student Council and the Highway Staff. She was voted "most likely to succeed, wittiest and most attractive." She played field hockey, tennis, basketball and badminton, was president of the Antiquity Club, vice president of the Debating Club, honorary chairman of the Science Fair, and a Foreign Travel Society Representative. Her girl friends reminisced in italicized notes: "Kitty's sunny disposition and terrific sense of humor make her one of the most popular girls in her class. No wonder the boys flock all the way from Pittsburgh to find out what goes on behind that flashing smile! She's impeccably groomed and marvelous at backgammon, and we'll long remember singing to the inspired accompaniment of her guitar. Her tennis game is great and she's a natural at languages. Her white Lincoln convertible has been the vehicle for many joyous outings. Those of us who have visited her lovely family home at Pierre Magnol plantation, in South Carolina, will forever remember Kitty as gracious mistress of her palatial estate." Behind the yearbook he found a leather-bound prize-winning essay his mother had written just before graduation: "Searching for a stage on which to enact the drama of free enterprise, American industry has evolved an architecture unique in the history of mankind: these magnificent towers of glass are the very soul of *Homo Americanus*. Yet once he has erected such noble structures, he still perseveres, never satisfied, never stopping

134

to enjoy the fruits of his labors. These buildings are America's greatest contribution to art, a monument to its restless energy."

Whalen turned back to the yearbook and continued leafing through it. In the final pages, he came across an advertisement. "Dollars—dollars—dollars: as graduates you need funds. Save as regularly as you eat or you will become financially undernourished. Open a checking and savings account, now, at any of the many branches of the Whalen Bank of Commerce and Savings. Don't procrastinate." Whalen hadn't realized that his father had owned a bank so long ago. He found his father's photograph on another advertisement and wondered if before his father and mother met, she might have seen it too. Whalen fantasized about his mother seeing his father for the first time while she was opening a savings account at his bank. But it occurred to him that his father had probably never been in half the branches, least of all the one advertised in the yearbook.

Whalen heard footsteps on the stairs. He turned towards the door. A tall young trooper entered pointing a gun at him. Whalen jumped to his feet.

"Don't you move, buddy. Get your hands up." He motioned with his gun and Whalen slowly raised his arms. "I found the other half," the trooper shouted to someone outside the door.

"I'll be right there," a voice answered from downstairs.

"There are two of us here, so don't try anything stupid," said the trooper.

"I wasn't going to," said Whalen.

A stocky sheriff brought the girl into the room. She looked disheveled, but when she saw Whalen with his arms over his head, she managed a smile.

"Search him," said the sheriff. The young trooper replaced his gun in his holster and moved towards Whalen. Whalen lowered his hands.

"I told you not to move, you fucker," yelled the trooper, stepping forward and slamming his fist into Whalen's face. Whalen staggered back, and the trooper pushed him up

136

against the wall. He pulled out the pockets of Whalen's pants and sniffed the fragments of dust in the lining.

"Now we're going outside," said the sheriff. He waved his gun towards the door.

The four of them walked slowly down the stairs; at the front door the trooper paused and turned off the lights before they walked outside, and stopped in front of Whalen's car.

"You left the key in the car. That's against the law."

"My car's in a private driveway. That's not against the law."

"Listen, smart ass, don't talk to me about the law." He turned to the trooper. "I'll drive these two back to the station. You bring the car."

The sheriff ordered Whalen and the girl to the rear seat of his car, and picked up the receiver of a buzzing short-wave radio. "Coming back with two robbery suspects. Male Caucasian, female Negro." Then he started the car and drove down the long driveway.

"Are we being arrested?" asked Whalen.

"What do you think?"

"But what for?"

"You'll find out first thing Monday morning. We don't book Sunday nights. You and your girl friend are going to spend the rest of the weekend as guests of our incorporated village."

They passed through the empty center of town. Whalen

remembered driving with his father along the same streets. "A proud town for proud people," his father had once said, pointing at the rows of new homes built for the Company's workers.

As they drove up, Whalen noticed that his car was already parked in front of the police station. The young trooper and a desk officer were waiting for them. "Can I see you alone for a moment?" Whalen asked the sheriff.

"Sorry," the sheriff answered. "Confessionals are closed now. That's why we stay open. You can talk here." The three policemen chuckled.

"I think you might be interested in what I have to say. But I don't want to tell you here," Whalen said quietly.

The sheriff extinguished his cigarette. "All right, but no tricks." They went to a small side room. "Now, what is it?"

"My name is Whalen. You saw it on my driver's license."

"Lot of Whalens in this country."

"Yes, I know. But my father was Horace Sumner Whalen."

The sheriff reached in his shirt pocket for another cigarette and smiled. "Sure. And your mother was Jacqueline Kennedy."

"No, please listen," said Whalen. "The house where you picked us up belongs to me. So does the park around it, and, for that matter, so does most of the land this town

138

and the Company are built on. The Town Hall was donated by my mother. There's even a family portrait in the lobby. I'm in it, standing next to my father. Go look."

"This township used to be called Whalenburg. If you're Whalen's son, why did you wait until now to tell us?"

"You didn't give me a chance," Whalen answered.

The sheriff got up slowly, puffing his cigarette.

"I'm entitled to a phone call, right?" Whalen continued. "Well, I've decided I would like to telephone the mayor. I want to tell him that I'm here. He'll be interested in knowing what happened to my face."

The sheriff stopped in front of him. "I know you're upset, Mr. Whalen," he said. "And you have good reason to be. I'm truly sorry all this happened. I'd be glad to—"

"You'd be glad to what?"

"My deputy and I will apologize."

"I don't feel offended. I just feel my face," said Whalen.

"We'll call a doctor. Or we can get you to a hospital right away."

"There's no need for that, but there is something else you can do for me."

"Sure. Anything, Mr. Whalen. I want to make up for this inconvenience."

"Good. Then I would like to pay back the deputy for my face. I'd like you to take care of it in front of me and my girl friend and the desk officer."

"What?"

"I think it's a fair exchange, sheriff. Otherwise I'll have to call the mayor—"

Without a word the sheriff stubbed out his cigarette and walked back to the other room. Whalen followed.

The girl sat close to the window and the trooper stood nearby. The desk officer was reading a newspaper. The sheriff stopped in the center of the room, glanced around and turned uneasily to his deputy. "Hey, Bob, come over here for a minute, would you?"

The deputy walked across the room and stood in front of the sheriff. The sheriff hesitated a moment, then swung his right fist into the trooper's face. The man staggered back. The desk officer jumped to his feet and went over to help the deputy, who was shaking, his lower lip cut and bleeding, his jaw turning red. The sheriff raised his hand: "Okay, Bob, that's it." He turned towards the desk sergeant and gestured at Whalen and the girl. "Drop the charges, Mike. They're leaving."

"Now in his letter, Mr. Howmet volunteers several suggestions. He does not think I should remain in a hotel. He thinks I should get myself a permanent home, perhaps

140

a town house in Pittsburgh, large enough for me to entertain my out-of-town friends. In case I should marry, it must be large enough for my wife, my children, possibly my grandchildren. He thinks I should either sell the country house or give it to Whalenburg to strengthen its ties with the Company. On the other hand, he feels I should retain the house in Watch Hill for the summer and the one in Palm Springs for the winter, but that I should dispose of the yacht and of the houses in Europe. He assumes that I might like to spend some time in the Company offices, either in Pittsburgh or in New York, getting acquainted, as he put it, with its inner workings, or that I might wish to enroll in the Yale Law School."

"Yes, Mr. Whalen. I am familiar with some of these recommendations, as the trustees expressed them at their last meeting."

"Then you might as well know what I think and what I want. The yacht and these houses should have been sold a long time ago. I don't want to live in Pittsburgh and I don't intend to work for the Company, because no matter where I began I would never master anything beyond the most immediate aspects of one department. No one man can possibly make sense of the whole operation. Furthermore, Mr. Howmet either doesn't know or doesn't remember that I left Yale just after I had entered."

"He might have assumed that you could make up for it now."

"I'm too old to make up for past failures. I don't want

141

to fit myself into any kind of structure. I want to live in Manhattan in a small apartment, no more than three or four rooms, in a building right on the East River, with windows facing the river and the heliport. Here is the address. Please make sure I have direct access to a boat."

"A boat?"

"Yes. I have placed an order for a small but fast boat. It sleeps two."

"If you'll excuse me, Mr. Whalen. Is there a marina near your apartment?"

"No. But the building is right on the bank, and I could easily get down to the water level with a rope ladder."

"It's against the law to pick up or discharge passengers at any unauthorized place on the East River."

"Too bad. The boat will be anchored in the midtown marina, and I'll hire someone to deliver it to the embankment in front of my house. He will also return it to the marina for me. There's a radiophone on board the boat so I can keep in touch with him."

"May I ask why you need such immediate access to the boat?"

"Why shouldn't I have it?"

"But the police—"

"Talk to the cops who manage not to see double-parked cars on Park Avenue."

"I'll do what I can."

"I want a space for my car in the garage, directly across from the exit."

"Your car?"

"A Ford. A twelve-cylinder Italian-made engine has been installed in place of the American one."

"Certainly, Mr. Whalen."

"Please have the apartment furnished. Anything functional will do. The maids, cook, chauffeur and two more people will live in a separate apartment on the floor below."

"Yes, Mr. Whalen. I should tell you that as you suggested. Executive Heliways, Inc. has been acquired by the Company."

"Good. I know some people there."

This list is from the Hall of Records. It contains about twenty-two thousand or so owners who currently hold title to property in this city. But the name of the owner might not be much help. Sometimes, a company or a person simply owns the land and the building on it. On the other hand, they may rent the building to a syndicate on a long-term lease. The syndicate in turn may have awarded an operating lease to another company which is itself owned by still another syndicate. Very often that second syndicate might be controlled by a conglomerate. As you see, Mr. Whalen, unless we assume that ownership is actual control, it's almost impossible to say who really owns that building.

Now let's take a look at the latest available tax assessments for the past year. In the left-hand column are the names of all the subsidiary companies and individuals who either own, lease or in some way control a property. Then we have the assessed land values. And over in this column is the total assessment of the land and buildings for tax purposes, since you must remember that in some instances real estate is assessed at less than sixty per cent of its actual value. And then of course we have the adjusted column reflecting the true market value.

Just before his death, your father realized the risks involved in owning real estate in rapidly deteriorating neighborhoods. As you may know, the city must legally take title to any property that falls four years behind on its taxes. There was no need to expand the Company's real-estate holdings, so your father relinquished some of the properties, that is, let the city take them over. It was a wise decision. The city then tried to unload the properties at public auctions, but most of them weren't sold. Now, the city instead of the Company has to maintain them. In some cases the city even had to reverse itself and offer us a sizable management fee just to keep open the buildings in which so many of our less fortunate citizens live.

I'm glad that Karen isn't living with me. I'd be frightened of her, afraid to turn my back on her, or close my eyes in her presence. I'd be afraid to express any emotion which could alienate her. I must appease her completely, just as I did my father.

I envy Karen's outbursts. She is never indifferent and never withdrawn, totally unpredictable. I've seen so many of her tantrums and repentances that when she swears it won't happen again, I can't believe her. She puts down my reliance on drugs without realizing that she's never without a vodka-on-the-rocks, and can't bear to be without a sun tan. I'm always anticipating the next blowup. Knowing that I feel this way bruises her self-confidence; my cynicism continuously undermines her faith in her own ability to master her moods.

When I know Karen is with Susan, I feel used, but today I took them both to lunch and now, a few hours later, I am absolutely calm.

The meal itself was unrelentingly depressing. Susan and Karen talked for an hour, while I sat silently eating my lunch as if I were invisible. But I feel as if I have finally faced something I've been avoiding for weeks and that the confrontation has ended my combined frenzy and lethargy.

They talked about sex. They talked about it as though they had never discussed it before. Susan said that very few people are sexually aware of themselves or of other people. Most people, she said, listen to what you say, but don't notice what you are trying to edit out or what remarks make you avert your eyes or gesture in a certain way. They don't look for sexual signals. Almost as if for my benefit Susan launched into a lecture about Karen's sensuality. She said that Karen's physical sense of herself is very strong, much stronger than her own, and that she picks up sexual feedback very quickly. She said she couldn't define what makes Karen so desirable or what draws people to her. Karen seemed surprised to hear that.

Susan said Karen is compellingly feminine, and that men and women are drawn to her by her elusiveness, by a desire to get to the passionate self beneath the cool exterior.

Then it was Karen's turn. She said that whenever she meets a new couple she tries to picture them in bed. Unlike herself, most people create sexual fantasies about other people only when they are not directly available.

As an afterthought Susan said that she finds some of

Karen's relationships with men incomprehensible. She explained that they fail because there seems to be no energy between Karen and her partners and she can't imagine them satisfying Karen. She didn't mention me but her point was obvious. "There is a kind of self-recognition completely lacking in most conventional relationships," Susan continued, looking at me. "It's sad," she added, "that so many people never have the chance to discover or fulfill themselves through another person."

Tonight Karen told me that she had been prowling naked around her apartment, watering her poor sodden plants, smoking one cigarette after another although her throat was raw, washing a dish or spoon as soon as she used it and from time to time glancing at poems. She had just discovered, she said, that the dry cleaner had lost the sash to her new St. Laurent robe. Then she hung up.

In the encounter group the blonde girl complained about my sarcasm. I said that it was just defensive humor, that I am sarcastic more to hide my real bitterness than to alienate or frighten anyone. I said that living is an arbitrary matter and that I have every right to renounce it. Every time I climbed a mountain in Katmandu I expected to die on the way up or on the way down; even now, whenever I drive anywhere, I don't expect to get where I'm going. No one in the group understood me.

Jeffrey said he couldn't comprehend how people can get angry with each other and then be reconciled. For him, the first sign of anger means that a relationship is over. Keith asked him if he wanted to talk about his conflict with me, but he didn't. I said, "This is absurd. Jeffrey has said he is completely indifferent to me and now you're all talking about our 'conflict.' " Jeffrey ignored my comment and went on talking about anger. Suddenly I was angry myself. For a few minutes I sat there hating him, about to explode, ready to walk over and hit him in the face. Then my anger changed to hurt. I felt as though I was suffocating, losing control; I wanted to leave. Joel said something to me, but I didn't even hear it. I was on the verge of shouting when Keith asked if I would come over to him. I screamed that I wouldn't. I could hear some of the people in the circle say, "Look, Jonathan, we're with you, we'll support you," and I shouted back, "No you won't. That isn't true," all the time wanting to say, "Please listen to me, please help me calm down."

Keith sat down beside me. Then Elizabeth sat next to me and handed me a cigarette. I puffed on it and apologized. "This is ridiculous." Someone said gently, "No. It's necessary."

My presence in the group has been important if only as a constant reminder that no one possesses completely consistent emotions. I can be described as neither a hostile nor a sympathetic person. My sense of myself is entirely relative. My hostility and sympathy vary, depending on whom I'm with: I compete or I pity. Either I'm not good enough for anyone or I'm too good for everyone. Being in the group has made me incredibly agitated. I want to give up contemplation and get out and move. Yet I am afraid that this energy is temporary, only a reaction to my feeling of entrapment within a static group. Every time we meet I become more aware of how dishonest we all are: we know our lives are chaotic, but we insist that everything happen in an orderly way and be logically conceived.

In the end I remain unfulfilled by our encounter performances. I feel that I have not confronted anything unknown. I told this to Karen and she accused me of expecting tangible changes from the sessions. In fact, all I want is honesty. Once when Karen did come to the group she was acting out her feelings and lay down on the floor sobbing. I pretended to comfort her. She tensed and pulled away to rejoin the circle, and I was left thoroughly embarrassed. Despite her angry screams I sensed that she too was somehow unmoved, cut off, aware that she was just playing a role. I knew that she protected herself by making herself believe no one else could ever really understand her. She displayed only the surface of her emotions, unable to plunge beyond everyday responses and gestures.

At a cocktail party given for me by Karen and Susan, I met a rather well-to-do man in his late forties. We talked about drugs and throughout our conversation he kept referring to opium as morphia. He spoke of young Americans as hashish-suckers and pipe-masticators. He invited me to dinner, and I accepted. We went to a Chinese restaurant, where he talked to the waiter in Mandarin. When I asked him where he'd picked it up, he joked that he hadn't learned it from a menu. He spoke about drug traffic, crudely insinuating that he had something to do with it. He gave me figures: a load of fifteen hundred pounds of pure uncut heroin, half the weight of an American sedan, costs eight million dollars in the "Golden Square": Burma, Laos, Thailand and Cambodia. Four weeks later, when it reaches the American market, its value is three hundred million. The stuff comes via American bases in Indochina, courtesy of bribed local officials and base commanders. He was proud of the history of his business and saw himself as a spiritual descendant of the eighteenth-century British who encouraged poppy-planting in India so that they could trade "black rice," as opium was called, with China. In fact, by that time Americans were also involved; they were accused by both the British and the French of being indiscriminately aggressive in their opium sale in China.

The man said he felt sorry for businessmen who have to work so hard for so little profit. He said he makes more money every year in his pursuit of happiness than my father did in a lifetime of Protestant grind. My father, he said, needed buildings and railroads and highways and towns and hundreds of thousands of workers; he had to negotiate with unions, promote politicians, brown-nose the people in power. By contrast, all this man needs is the short-term co-operation of a few U.S. flight sergeants, some customs men, and a few narcotics detectives.

He knows of my experiences in Burma and India and would like to have one of his associates talk to me.

You may have noticed in today's paper that the police are very proud of themselves for discovering a two-hundred-and-fifty-pound heroin stash. They claimed the street value was close to forty million dollars. Of course, the police exaggerate because it makes them look more efficient. Let's be conservative and say the stuff was only worth fifteen million. Think of it. A suitcase in the trunk of a Ford worth fifteen million dollars.

You may think heroin-dealing is a dirty, vicious business, Mr. Whalen, but you yourself are in an equally corrupt enterprise. The fish caught near the outwash of one of your father's factories are unfit to eat because their flesh has been contaminated by nickel. Workers in your smelters, mines and plating factories have been poisoned by the same stuff as the fish. Their livers are damaged; they suffer from high blood pressure, hardening of the arteries and arthritis. So how about talking business, and throwing all your humanity crap to the diseased fish?

Now, Whalen, I'm not responsible for hundreds of thousands of people who use spoons, tinfoil and needles to hit themselves with the dope I deal. I don't make them do it. You know that; you were once an addict yourself. The man in the black overcoat who gives kiddies free samples is Madison Avenue shit. Why should I give away free samples when I can sell every bag I have?

Your father made it a practice to keep up with the very latest in industrial technology. You will be pleased to know, Mr. Whalen, that we have purchased the newest high-speed computer, known as system 1001 Model 40. This computer system, which will require a whole building to house it, is capable of storing eight hundred million bits of data. That's more information than is contained in every book ever written. Model 40 can execute an instruction in one-hundred-billionth of a second and print out two thousand lines of complex information per minute. Hard to imagine, isn't it?

This is the first time I have really tried to allow someone else to know me. And yet now Karen is as inaccessible emotionally as she was physically all those years I was away. When days go by and I don't see or hear from her our relationship begins to seem like fantasy.

Since she is at least partly aware of my reaction, it is difficult for me not to interpret her silence as an intentional weakening of our connection. I'm beginning to suspect that she is clinging to a false image of me which she formed while I was away, and which she doesn't want altered. I refuse to be the persona of Karen's imagination.

Whenever I was involved with a woman, I assumed she would protect me, but Karen is afraid of taking responsibility for me or for our relationship. She hates it when I visit her without advance warning or show her I'm dependent on her. She refuses to give me access to the areas of her life in which I'm not already involved. I'm not allowed to read her diary or her letters or to meet most of the people she sees. I remember her warning me not to "burn my bridges." What bridges? To where? To Rangoon, to Bombay, or to the clinic in Munich? I have nowhere left to cross to. On the other hand, she always keeps open a number of escape routes. All my energy is required to keep my various selves together for her.

Karen thinks I oversimplify, that we should not depend

on each other to the same extent. She says we're more complicated than our most elaborate camouflages.

The encounter group has become predictable. Nothing seems exciting or new any more, least of all our presentations of self. This is especially so with me, since my performances are anecdotal and rehearsed.

Yesterday my temperature hit 104°. The fever has gone now but my eyes are still tired and my body aches; I've been in bed for three days unable to move, to read, or to think.

I've had these symptoms before: once when I was about to leave the country and once in India after my mother's detectives found me. It's not as terrifying now. I used to be gripped by panic, but now my body refuses to give in completely. Wednesday was the worst day. My heart raced and I could barely feel my pulse. Then my blood pressure dropped and I had difficulty breathing, but the next moment I was calm and no longer felt the need for a doctor. Part of me refused to become engaged and remained fascinated by my own terror.

I wanted to call Karen but I felt drained. Thoughts that have barely been present for the past few months began to reappear. I remembered the fantasy of my father that I nourished as a child. I imagined him visiting his employees and having supper in their homes. I told myself that I was lucky to have such an important father even though it meant he'd never have enough time for me because there were so many men and women and children to be taken care of. I could never expect to compete with every smoking chimney in Pennsylvania. I never admitted that because I was just one child he hadn't cared about me at all.

Even if he were alive today, he would have no idea who I am. I don't think he could answer a simple questionnaire about my height or my childhood illnesses. He certainly would know nothing about my tastes, my friends, or my mind. And what would he who refused to travel to any country that did not have business relations with American industry say about my years abroad.

I want to learn more about my father and my family

and to meet the old partners who knew and respected him for most of their lives. I hope I will not cause them or the Company any embarrassment.

During the past days I have had a recurring physical sensation. It is as if the world were very sharply defined, but at the same time remote. Objects vibrate and quiver against me, but I cannot touch them. It's like coming into bright sunlight from a photographer's darkroom. I fear that this sensation will last forever, that I will never be able to explain it and that I'm the only one who feels it.

Tibetans have based an entire culture on death and the various states following it. They have symbols and a language that convey what it is like to die, and what one feels and thinks while being dead.

In Nepal, a Tibetan refugee told me that he had died many times before emerging as his present self. He said that when death again approaches, he will choose his future parents and the place of his forthcoming birth and will pass this information on to others. After his body dies, a search will be conducted to find the child who is his reincarnation. The child who recognizes his belongings from a previous life will be acknowledged as his reincarnated self.

Our language has no words to express such alien concepts as the event of death or afterlife.

He rolled down the window, and the sharp wind blew rain against his face. The car rocked to right and left in time with the swaying elms which arched high above the road. In front of him the highway and the alley of trees seemed to disappear into darkness. Whalen stopped the car. He got out and walked towards the forest.

He wrapped his coat tighter around him. Within the shelter of the forest, the ground was dry and sandy, but high above him the wind continued to snap the treetops back and forth. Protected from the rain as if by a roof and walls, he could hear grasshoppers chirping in the tall field grass.

The sound fascinated him. He had found the one calm place in the midst of the storm, a quiet voice calling him to the earth.

In this part of the country people are kinda patriotic, know what I mean? About two years ago when domestic-car sales went down, things got rough for foreign-car owners. If you drove anything but an American car into a gas station, the attendant might just slip a couple of sugar cubes into your gas tank, courtesy of Detroit, you might say. Little bugs got sick soon after they swallowed that sugar; they coughed and spit and puffed. Drivers couldn't locate the trouble and mechanics couldn't repair the engines once they sugar-coated the innards. So you were smart to bury that twelve-cylinder immigrant under a Ford hood.

I been bird-watching for years. A European cuckoo comes to America and gets a nice nest but it can't get food by itself. No, sir, it's too lazy, and it knows our birds can't stand to see another one suffer. And so pretty soon other birds give it their food, even though they might be hungry themselves.

Take American cuckoos. They ain't on welfare. They feed themselves and build their own nests. Sure sometimes they have to live in nests left by other birds and every so often they throw out the old eggs, but once they've got a nest they stick to it, they improve it, they raise a family and even bring in other birds to live with them.

The summer was ending. The leaves had not yet turned but the air already gave off a scent of vegetable decay. Layers of thin grey clouds hung low over the woods, over the highways, over the buildings, over the billboards. The fog broke for a moment to reveal the peaks of skyscrapers, then closed in again.

Whalen drove beside the river, past the bridge and the railroad station. He parked his car in a nearby lot and got out. He scanned the riverbank until he found the spot he was looking for, then walked down the embankment and stood at the water's edge.

One winter night years ago he and Peter, one of his grade-school friends, had decided to cross the river even though it was full of ice. Through the folds of thick fog they could see an occasional light flickering on the far shore. Jonathan untied one of the abandoned old boats anchored at the nearby pier; Peter jumped in and sat in the stern clutching two crude oars. Then Jonathan slid onto the ice at the river's edge and climbed aboard. The boat shuddered as the current seized it and carried it away from shore. Jonathan braced his legs, dipped the oars awkwardly into the water, and frantically heaving his body back and forth, tried to row the boat across the swollen river. They kept colliding with chunks of ice large and solid as boulders. In the darkness the jagged ice tore at the trembling boat, which was moving rapidly down-stream. Soon they no longer saw any shore lights and realized that the boat had already passed the pier and was on its way to the ocean.

Jonathan's temples were pounding and the wind chilled the sweat on his forehead. Knowing he could no longer control the boat made him reckless, almost giddy, and his hands loosened their grip on the oars. Peter sensed his surrender; Jonathan heard him scream. Suddenly a huge wave sloshed over the side of the boat, washing Jonathan into the water. Blades of ice cut his arms and face, and he expected one of them to slit his throat. He drifted rapidly for some time, until his body slammed into a jetty. He heaved himself out of the water. Peter was right behind him but seemed to have given in to the water, for his body was limp as Jonathan pulled him from the river. Peter collapsed on the wet stone, and Jonathan had to drag him through a field and a dense thicket until they reached the highway, where the neon sign of a gas station glowed through the fog about two hundred yards down the road.

When Jonathan stumbled into the gas station, the attendant looked up from his newspaper only long enough to nod at them. Jonathan laid Peter on the ground, tore off Peter's frozen jacket, shirt, trousers and waterlogged boots. The attendant finally realized he had to do something when he saw Peter stripped naked. In the back of the garage he found a greasy paint tarpaulin and they wrapped Peter in it and carried him into the office. Then the attendant called the police.

He drove farther on. By dawn he was passing meadows and ponds. He turned off the main highway and continued along a marsh road by the edge of the woods. The rising sun was dispersing the mist that hung over the fields. On both sides of the road he saw houses and shacks, most of them abandoned. Shutters had fallen off the houses or swung by a single hinge, roofs sagged over crumbling walls and ruined chimneys rose above masses of broken bricks. The car's wheels churned slowly in the sand when he drove back to the highway. Banks of scrub pine grew beside the road, and the green needles filtered the sun and dappled his car's hood. He felt totally invisible behind the wheel.

"Now let's say you have a car and it's got a stock rear end, right? You jack up both rear tires of the car, you put the transmission in high gear and rev the engine up to the speed of one hundred miles per hour. You let one wheel down on the ground and keep the other up in the air. What happens?"

"I don't know. I don't think I could ever figure it out."

"I knew you couldn't. All you young people know is when you're hungry or sleepy or horny. But I'll tell you anyhow. Putting one wheel down on the ground makes the one in the air revolve at two hundred miles per hour and the speedometer shows half the speed of the wheel in the air. You get it? Anybody who really knew his stuff would get that."

"He says the car overheats. It idles bad when it's hot and doesn't accelerate right."

"Well, take a look at the radiator. If it's okay, check the belts and the pump."

"I did all that. I even put in a new gasket for the intake manifold. Now he's back and says the same thing's happening again."

The mechanic walked over to Whalen. "Well," he said, "the only other thing it could be is vapor lock. Sometimes the heat under the hood makes the gas evaporate in the fuel line. What we may have to do is install a bigger fuel pump. You know these Italian engines are temperamental; they're not built for everyday driving. You ever tried working on one?"

"That's not my job. All I want is for you to fix my car so I can get where I'm going."

"Well, that may take a while. We'll have to order the new pump. These engines are so rare we don't bother keeping parts in stock."

"But I want it now."

"I don't think we can do it."

"You have to. Otherwise—"

"Otherwise, what?"

"Otherwise, my lawyers will pressure you, you'll overheat and your business will evaporate."

"Jonathan, you don't realize how difficult it is to find reliable executives. If we want to hold onto our best men, or avoid forcing them into costly rotation within our departments, we must aim at providing optimal selective employment.

"For example, here are some facts about the candidates we recently interviewed for an important executive spot: eighty per cent had some disorder in the urinary tract and anal zones and admitted having sexual problems ranging from inadequate erection to complete impotence. More

165

than forty per cent complained of heart palpitation, tension, breathing difficulties or headaches. We established that close to ninety per cent of these otherwise outstanding businessmen had psychic complaints which included anxiety, insomnia, depression, forgetfulness, sweating and ulcers. We obtained this information through the use of highly sophisticated scientific testing and multidimensional personality analysis and by maintaining top-level security lists which contain independently acquired information about an applicant's health, family, habits, etc., etc. Your father was always in favor of this 'anti-ulcer' policy. He was ahead of his time, Jonathan."

"Then he should have hired Peruvian Indians. They never develop ulcers."

"Peruvian Indians?"

"Yes. But, apparently they lack ambition, don't compete, and don't plan ahead."

"Jonathan, it's too bad but we have people like that right here in this country. All on welfare."

A plump man with a neatly folded newspaper stood next to him on the street corner. The man absent-mindedly tapped the pavement with his large black umbrella as he waited for the light to change. A woman waited beside them. She wore a cloth coat and ankle socks. She had set down her shopping bags on the sidewalk, and was rummaging through her handbag for a scarf, he supposed, or one of those accordion-pleated plastic rain hats.

The light turned green. They crossed the street three abreast, then went single file down the subway entrance, bought their tokens and pushed through the turnstiles. Whalen stayed close to the woman. She ambled towards the front of the platform and put a coin into a gum machine. No gum came out. She inserted another coin. Still nothing happened. Then she forgot the gum and concentrated on the dirty mirror above the machine. She was a little too short and had to stretch to see her whole face. She pushed some stray wisps of hair into place, then walked to a bench and sat down, arranged her bags around her and rubbed her eyes with wrinkled, arthritic fingers. The subway rumbled in the distance. People on the platform shifted their weight, buttoned or unbuttoned their coats, smoothed their hair, looked at their watches, gathered their packages together, pressed their umbrellas to their sides. He felt a sudden draft, and small particles of dirt stirred up by the train settled on him as it roared to a stop and the doors hissed open.

He stepped into the subway and hurried to a cold pink plastic seat. As the train jolted forward he settled back with his eyes closed, trying not to think. His stomach was hollow and cold, and his heart felt as if it were in a vice. He held his breath and braced himself against the subway's rocking to ease the enormous throb in his chest. The train stopped, panted for a moment, and then continued. He sat rigid, counting the stops.

Whalen hurried through the lobby of his hotel, his clothes dripping water on the carpet and on the elevator floor. Once inside his room he ripped off his wet clothes and threw them in the bathtub. He put on dry things but was still shivering with cold. He drank a glass of cognac and went down to experience what Karen called "the throbbing of the hotel lobby."

It was late. The lobby was almost empty. There was a man at the cashier's window, an elderly woman talking on the house phone, and a plump man reading a newspaper. He was just about to enter the bar when he realized that he'd seen the plump man on the subway. As Whalen glanced at him again, the man raised his paper as if to hide behind it. His black umbrella was propped against the chair beside him.

Whalen decided to find out if the man was following him. He went upstairs. When he returned with a raincoat thrown over his shoulder, the man was still reading his paper. Whalen went to the cashier's window, changed a fifty-dollar bill and strolled casually out of the lobby. The doorman promptly came over to him and Whalen asked for a taxi. The plump man didn't move as the doorman hailed a cab and opened the door. As the cab left the curb, Whalen turned to look into the lobby again. The man was still there, but two large sedans which had been parked opposite the hotel immediately pulled out behind the taxi. Whalen asked the driver to go around the block. The taxi turned the corner, and the two cars followed. He told the driver to take the first right turn and then the next left. The cars were still behind him.

When the taxi driver got nervous, Whalen explained that he had bet some friends that he could lose them in city traffic, but the driver looked incredulous. Whalen asked to be dropped in the middle of Yorkville, and as the taxi halted, he jumped out and headed into the densest part of the crowd. He ducked behind a newspaper stand and peered back. Both cars had pulled to the curb. Two men in raincoats got out of each car and went off in different directions. As one of them passed the stand, Whalen could hear the static of the walkie-talkie the man

169

was carrying. Whalen mingled with people lined up to buy cigarettes and newspapers. His clothes were soaked again; he quickly moved into a crowded cafeteria and sat at a table away from the window with his back to the street.

He wondered who could afford such an elaborate setup: the man who followed him on the subway, two cars, four more men equipped with walkie-talkies. He didn't think it was the police. They might suspect he had talked business with the drug dealers who came to see him but they'd soon realize he wasn't dealing. What if he was being tailed by the drug people? He thought about newspaper stories of attempts to kidnap rich children, then dismissed them; anyone who wanted to kidnap him would probably be more subtle and efficient.

The coffee he'd drunk was too weak. He felt sluggish. He thought of calling Karen, then decided against it. He knew what would happen. Now, when they talked on the phone, she sounded distant, witty, ironic and cold. It was bad enough being trapped in Yorkville by the rain and the pursuers without being trapped by her voice.

Karen and I talked about sex and anger. She said that for her the two are inextricably related. She feels that if a man really wants to get to her, she should make it as difficult as possible. That's why she keeps her nails long, she says, to be able to scratch and claw.

She talked about her parents' violent arguments. One ended with her father shouting at the top of his lungs: "Any whore in Denver is better in bed than you are!" To which her mother replied: "I'm glad you can get it up for the whores in Denver."

She said she wanted to get up and call me last night because she was tense and frustrated and still turned on. She was glad we had made love; her tension had disappeared and she had fallen asleep almost immediately. For Karen, love is a powerful drug. She still claims that I'm sexually guarded, so she must also pretend to be cold or risk scaring me off. This makes her feel like a Victorian woman whose slightest sexual request was considered an aberration. She accuses me of wanting her to be completely passive, to ask for nothing, ready to accept sex whenever I want to give it.

Her main objective is someday to make me completely lose control in love-making and in life. She says I am passionless and self-contained, that I have limited emotions with no extremes of anger, happiness or sorrow. I lost them somewhere abroad, she says, as if I had them before I left.

The desk clerk telephoned that a man was on his way up. "He told me he has an interview with you, Mr. Whalen."

"Yes, that's right," said Whalen.

A balding, slightly stooped man in his forties entered the room and hesitantly extended his hand.

Whalen shook it. "I want you to cook for me and my friends," he said.

"Yes, sir, I understand." The man looked at him. "Would you like to see my credentials and letters of reference?"

"You can leave them with me. But if you want to, tell me briefly where you worked before."

The man smiled. "I've worked in many places, sir. I

went to the Hotel School and graduated in cooking, service and restaurant management. I spent three years working at the Beau Rivage in Lausanne, and the Hotel de L'Etrier in Crans. Later I became Chef de Cuisine at the Prince Royal Hotel at Bourg-Léopold, then Chef de Garde at the Hotel Palace in Madrid. After that I was a Captain at Le Pavillon in New York, and then I worked for a year as a purchasing agent for the Restaurant Associates chain. Then I went back to France, where I lectured in the cooking section of L'Ecole Professionnelle du Rhône."

"I guess that's all right," said Whalen.

The man went on. "The last three years I worked for Mrs. Robert Allcott the Third. I've a letter of recommendation from her. And before that I was in the employ of Mrs. Charlotte Cobb-McKay and before—"

"Is there anything else?" Whalen asked.

"Well, sir—" The man's French accent became more noticeable. "There's nothing in the field of *haute cuisine* that I can't do. But of course—" he paused—"of course, you can't compare what I could cook for you, let's say, in Paris or in Crans, to what I can prepare in New York or Hobe Sound. Here, freezing kills the flavor."

Whalen cut in. "You are single, aren't you?"

"I am separated from my wife. She and my children live in France."

"All right," said Whalen. "Now, as my lawyers discussed with your agent, I'm ready to pay you three thousand dollars a month. You will have free time only when I am not in town or when I'm dining out. Otherwise you will have to be immediately available."

"Yes, sir," said the man. "Will I be living on the premises?"

"Yes, you will," said Whalen. "I've hired two maids. One will take care of the dishes and kitchen. The other one will look after the apartment. They are both Swiss. You'll like them, I'm sure."

"Thank you, sir," said the man. He paused a moment before leaving. "My former employer, Mrs. Allcott, often talked about your parents, sir. She admired them greatly."

"They are both dead, now," said Whalen.

"Yes, sir, I know that. I am sorry."

In the rear-view mirror he saw the car following him and stepped on the accelerator. The car lurched forward. He passed two trucks and when he saw that there was no approaching traffic on the other side of the highway, he decided to make a U turn. He jerked the steering wheel to the left and as the car leaned to one side he pulled out the hand brake, using it to lock the rear wheels. The car spun to the left, skidding and pitching as if it were being lifted by a giant crane. In an instant, his direction was completely reversed. He swung the steering wheel to the right and released the hand brake, simultaneously depressing the gas pedal again. The front of the car swayed, then stabilized. He saw the pursuing car braking on the other side of the highway, its tires squealing as he passed it, and he knew they couldn't possibly catch him now. He sped on for about a mile, turned at an intersection and continued speeding for another mile. He slowed down, parked his car at the curb and turned off the engine. He could hear the faint siren of a police car far away.

Whalen walked around the room, glancing at the modern paintings, and paused at the window. He looked out at the streets and buildings of Manhattan spread below him like an architect's model.

"I remember looking down at the street from my father's office when I was a child. I could open the window—"

"Oh, yes," said Macauley. "The old-fashioned windows." He came closer and stood next to Whalen. "Your father's office was on the top floor of the old Coinage Building, wasn't it?" He gestured downtown.

"No. On the twenty-fifth."

Macauley returned to his desk. It was enormous, full of miniature screens, buttons, knoos and flickering lights. He noticed Whalen looking at it. "I had this installed recently," Macauley said, patting the desk affectionately. "It's made of hand-rubbed walnut. It has a multi-system TV. You can watch eight channels at the same time. Next to it is a closed-circuit TV, hooked up with the videophone, and a video-cassette player and monitor so I can watch myself talking to people. I can even freeze a single frame and create an instant portrait of myself." He laughed. "And this one"—he pointed to the right—"is a conference telephone with hand-free speakers and an electronic touch dial coupled to video so I can see whomever I'm talking to. Here, farther to the right, we have a twelve-digit memory calculator connected with our central corporate data bank. Every business figure of the last twenty-five years is retrievable in a split second as if from a giant book. And here special gauges compute the working time and wear on every instrument. Your father would have loved it. Don't you think so, Jonathan?" Whalen nodded. Macauley continued. "In only forty-five seconds this telecopier can transmit over telephone or radio a facsimile of a document or color photograph,

176

either across the corridor of this building or across the Atlantic or Pacific. Here, on the left, is my personal ticker tape. Quotations of our stock, and of our affiliates, come across in unusually bright yellow. Over here, in the center, are the intercom, the Dictaphones, and the paging systems, data-retrieval subset and—"

"It all seems very complicated."

"It certainly is, Jonathan. But so is our business. When your father was running this Company, he was greatly in favor of introducing the latest methods of speeding up production. We go further: we speed up business communications. Without some of our products the astronauts might not have walked on the moon. Today this Company is a vast conglomerate with over forty national and worldwide subsidiaries. Metals, once your father's major interest, are now only our fourth-largest area. We are in aerospace, pharmaceuticals, computers, food, coal mining, gas turbines, offshore drilling, television, semiconductors, insurance, realty development, publishing, and dozens of other industries—from prostaglandins to prefabricated, prefurnished housing. In terms of sales we rank among the top ten largest industrial corporations of this country." Again he pointed at his desk, grinning. "Come to think of it, your father wouldn't approve of it: this desk is foreign-made. But he would like the wood. It's American walnut. Now, Jonathan, do sit down and tell me what brings you here?"

Whalen sat down and looked up at Macauley, who

remained leaning against his desk. "I'm being followed around the clock by several men," Whalen said calmly. "They carry walkie-talkies and tail me whenever I drive."

Macauley's expression did not alter. "How do you know that?" he asked.

"I've seen them. I managed to lose them once, you see. Now they're back again. They're probably downstairs waiting for me."

"Why are you telling me this?"

"I wanted to find out whether you know anything about it."

Macauley looked at him intently. "I think it's time to be frank with you, Jonathan. You're being followed, protected, rather, by order of this Company and its shareholders. You have been under constant surveillance since you landed in New York. I would have told you about it soon, anyhow—"

"But why?"

"Because you're the sole inheritor of your family's vast holdings; you're one of this Company's major shareholders. You represent several—"

"But I didn't ask you to protect me," Whalen interrupted.

"Correct. We arranged it after being encouraged and authorized by Mr. Walter Howmet, one of your father's closest friends and one of your former trustees. Like you, Howmet is a major shareholder. He appreciated our predicament."

"When I came into my inheritance a few days ago, Mr. Howmet's trusteeship ended—"

"I know that, Jonathan. However, the board of directors, realizing how vulnerable you are, was afraid that through you the Company might also become vulnerable."

Whalen got up, went to the window, and returned to his seat. "How am I vulnerable?" he asked.

"Try to understand, Jonathan. Down there"—Macauley pointed towards the windows—"are men who murder people for a fee. Who shoot a man simply to get his wallet. Who steal teen-agers' bikes and slash their victims' eyes to prevent identification. Don't you know that you are in the midst of all this? You're their prey." Macauley opened a bar in his desk and pointed at the row of gold-topped crystal decanters. "Can I give you anything?" Whalen shook his head. Macauley poured himself a drink. "I am responsible to my partners, to our clients here and abroad and to our shareholders. If something should happen to you—and it could if you aren't protected—it would affect all of us. This Company cannot afford such a risk."

"Why don't you have me stored in the Company's vault?"

Macauley laughed loudly. "Now, don't be bitter, Jonathan."

"Why wasn't I asked? Why wasn't I even told?"

"Good question. I take the responsibility for that. I was

afraid it would frighten you. Before you arrived we didn't know much about you, and what we did know—"

"What did you know?"

"The trustees have always indicated that your life style is, shall we say, unpredictable. Apparently you have come quite close to death—"

"My father went swimming during a storm. He drowned. My mother, I'm told—"

"In any case, you were away from home for so many years that we assumed you would find New York, as well as Pittsburgh, quite alien. We had good reason to fear for you. Mind you, the Company has absorbed the cost of this protection, and will continue to absorb it."

"How much does it cost to tail me around the clock?"

"I don't have the exact figures on hand. In any case it's a necessary expense."

"Speaking as a shareholder I think you are wasting the Company's money. Are you also checking my friends? Recording my conversations? Videotaping my girl friends when they screw me?"

Macauley laughed again. "I can tell you've already seen some movies about our gangster underworld. All we care about, Jonathan, is your personal safety. We managed to suppress any explicit news coverage: the press didn't know about your return to America, and the conditions of your family trust were never made public. We intend to continue ensuring your safety."

180

"I am going to hire my own protection. I'll let you know when I do."

"All right. If you think it's best. If I can be of any help, Jonathan, please call."

"Thank you, I will." Whalen got up, and Macauley escorted him to the door. "The Howmets are very eager to see you, Jonathan," he said, shaking Whalen's hand. "Have they managed to get in touch with you?"

"I'm seeing them tomorrow," Whalen said, as he walked through the door. A woman was waiting for him in the outer office.

"Mr. Whalen? I'm Mr. Macauley's secretary. May I take you down in his private elevator?"

"To those of us who knew and loved her, your mother's death came as a terrible shock. Even those of us who were not so fortunate as to be her intimate friends—she did not have many, you know—will always remember—" Mrs. Howmet paused, sipped her tea, then continued. "The twinkle in her eye, her smile and her laughter, her refinement! Your mother was so deep, so sincere, she shared so many of her interests with me, and taught me to appreciate the finer things in life." She sipped her tea and rang for a servant.

"Mrs. Howmet—" interrupted Whalen.

"Please call me Helen. I held you when you were a baby." She beamed.

"Helen, have you ever seen the Bowery?"

"Bowery? What is that?"

"That's an area in downtown New York. Not too far from Wall Street."

"No, Jonathan. We almost never drive through the city."

"Well, hundreds of derelicts live there. They beg for food and sleep on the street and many of them die without any relief. I thought that our Company might try to help them, give them a hospital, maybe permanent care."

A maid brought fresh tea. Mrs. Howmet was listening attentively. "Go on, Jonathan."

"After all, they are part of our community. As I said, within walking distance of our offices."

"But Jonathan, the Company should not attempt such an arbitrary interference in other people's lives," said Mrs. Howmet. "The aim of private industry has never been to force others to do what they don't want to do."

"These people don't know what's good or bad for them," said Whalen. "Even their sores don't heal. In the Middle Ages they would at least have been put into poor-

182

houses. Today they starve. They're diseased. They die right in the midst of the traffic. The Peruvian Indians live better than these people. Meanwhile, one of our subsidiaries introduces a new after-shave lotion and spends eleven million dollars advertising it in the first six months. The Company donates hundreds of thousands of dollars to some of the already well-endowed art galleries and museums. Just recently it gave two hundred thousand dollars to the Evidence of Human Soul Society."

Mrs. Howmet leaned towards him and gently touched his hand. "I haven't seen you for many years, Jonathan, but I've always felt you were the child Walter and I never had, so I think I can be frank. You have traveled a lot and due to your painful past experiences you are easily influenced. The Company is not our private property. It belongs to thousands and thousands of shareholders, to decent men and women who have worked all their lives. We are all conscious of human misery, and it has always been the Company's policy, just as it was your father's and my husband's, to help those who want to help themselves. The soul is of vital interest to the human race. Our museums preserve the best expressions of the soul. Giving money to the derelicts benefits no one, not even the derelicts themselves. They go on sleeping on the streets and stealing to satisfy their diseased appetites. In this country there are millions of people who need all the help industry can give them, because they are willing to offer something in return. Industry helps them and it needs them."

"But if it is up to the shareholders," Whalen insisted, "and if Mr. Howmet and I could address them—"

"You talk like a child, Jonathan. Life isn't Hollywood. What would your father have said to all this! And my husband!" Her voice became somber. "Don't even discuss it with Walter. He is strongly principled. Do you honestly believe that if it were the right thing to do he would not have taken care of your unfortunates ages ago? But it's not right, it's not, Jonathan. Please believe me."

"But some of those derelicts, the stronger ones, try to work. When a car stops for a red light, they try to clean the windshield."

She got up and looked at him pleadingly. "Be reasonable. The windshield, indeed! Now listen to me carefully." Whalen stood up and she walked with him around the room, her hand on his arm. Her voice was almost a whisper now. "Walter will talk to you about joining an Order to which both he and your father belonged. He'll tell you everything you need to know about it. All I want to say is that it is important that you join it, important for you and for all of us." She paused, smiled and continued. "Oh, yes, a minor point. I think you ought to get a good haircut and some new clothes. After all, you're settled now." She stopped and listened to noises outside the room. "I think Walter is home. He's very anxious to see you and talk to you. I'll leave you two alone."

I've been a bodyguard since I was twenty-two. I've worked for businessmen, for movie and television people, for politicians. I saved the lives of at least four of my clients. I've failed only a couple of times. One died at an opening night in the middle of a black-tie crowd in a theater lobby. He was injected with a deadly chemical right through his clothes. Even I thought it was a heart attack. The second client was hit at the curb while walking from his office building to his car. The bullet came from a slow-moving car in the morning rush traffic. When he fell, I assumed the assassin had fired from a skyscraper but now I know the killer was a sharpshooter in a stolen car. His accomplice was at the wheel; he hid in the car's trunk and aimed through a hole just large enough to accommodate the rifle barrel and silencer.

But most cases aren't so extreme. Recently I met a girl I liked. One day I invited her to my apartment for dinner. We planned to eat early, then drive to my beach house for the weekend. We were in the middle of dinner when I got a phone call from a former client who wanted to talk to me about some unfinished business. I had to leave the girl.

When I returned two hours later, she was gone; she had left a nasty note. I was upset, but I drove to the shore anyway and spent the weekend by myself. When I returned to the city, I called her, and as if nothing had happened invited her to my apartment again. She also seemed to have forgotten the incident and accepted. She arrived on time. After two drinks, I showed her a photo album of female models, escorts, night-club performers, masseuses and so on, all available for hire. In some photographs the girls were nude and in very crude poses. I passed the album to her. "What makes you think you're superior to these girls?" I asked her. She looked through the album calmly, put it aside, got up and went to the bathroom. I turned on the television and waited for her to come out. After a while it occurred to me that she was taking a long time. I went to the bathroom door and listened: not a sound. I called her name; no answer. I turned the knob, but the door was locked. I ordered her to open it. No reply. I called her again. Again no answer. I finally forced the lock with a screw driver. She was sprawled naked on the floor with both arms hanging over the edge of the bathtub. The hot water was already red with her blood. Her wrists were sliced apart so wide that a layer of pale fat hung down like ripped-out lining. Her face was completely white; she didn't react when I shouted her name. What would you do in that situation, Mr. Whalen? Could you trust any doctor to take her to the hospital without reporting the accident to the police? To newsmen? Photographers?

But then, of course, you're the major shareholder in the Company. The Company has not only many competitors, but also many enemies, inside and out. For instance, it's investing in a device which converts exhaust fumes into carbon dioxide and water vapor, right? The Company hopes that domestic and foreign car makers will buy enough of the converters to make the expansion pay. But many of the shareholders and many of the Company's subsidiaries know that several large engine manufacturers, including Detroit car makers, are ready to manufacture their own superior and cheaper purification devices. So they think the catalytic-converter progam should be scrapped to prevent the Company and its shareholders serious losses.

And what about prostaglandins? Here's a fantastic drug which can cure and arrest glaucoma, arthritis, intestinal ulcers, certain heart and kidney ailments. What's more, it can also be marketed as a method of birth control. All the major pharmaceutical companies have been working on prostaglandins for almost twenty years. Now, only five years ago your Company enters this field, commits enormous resources to research and, who knows, maybe even does a little spying on the competitors' research. It's no wonder that last week Mr. Macauley informed the stockholders that one of the Company's major subsidiaries is ready to start world marketing of the drug, at least two years ahead of anyone else. Do you realize that this means disaster for many competitors? I don't have to tell you, then, why you personally might become, or probably already are, a factor in other people's plans. Blackmail, revenge, scandal, you name it.

A minor point, in case you decide to hire me. I know that you don't plan to take a regular job and that you intend to remain unattached. To protect you I can't be limited to just a few hours. I must be with you or next to you as often as needed, during the day, the evening or at night.

You must never pay me in advance, Mr. Whalen. What I'm saying is that I'll know more about your life than anyone else around you. That's why I could conceivably be the person most likely to sell you out. I'm telling you this because sooner or later it would occur to you anyway. If you're harmed, you must assume that I plotted it. If you're killed, I should be your estate's prime suspect.

When I was a student I showed my mother a photograph of Karen leaning against me in the courtyard of my college. My mother looked at it carefully and remarked that I was very handsome but that the courtyard's hedges needed trimming. Already she refused to acknowledge Karen.

I chartered a yacht, and Karen and I spent the evening gliding noiselessly around Manhattan. The yacht seemed like a prop floating on a gigantic water stage. At the mouth of the Hudson we moved between two transatlantic ships, one departing and one about to dock. Their passengers looked down and watched as we were served dinner on deck. Karen talked about her encounter group and about her conviction that people didn't want to interact with her. Her last group session centered around an affair she once had; Susan played her boy friend. Before the drama began Susan had been afraid that she wouldn't be able to play the boy friend well. She claimed she didn't want to be in the scene at all, but because of her loyalty to Karen she couldn't refuse.

After the fitting, my tailor asked if I liked porno movies. I told him I did sometimes. He offered me some grass and began talking about the movie and TV stars he'd fitted. Everyone else had gone home and I was alone with him. He'd sent for some additional fabric samples and suggested that we watch a porno right then while we waited for the fabrics to arrive. I got slightly high and agreed. For some reason the film was upside down and he didn't know how to fix it without damaging the film, so we sat there watching an upside-down Scandinavian stag film. Then he propositioned me. I was mildly interested, even though I knew he was a phony who would probably jerk off and then lie to his customers about how good in bed I was. I probably could have gotten involved, but something about the scene upset me. I decided to leave and mumbled some story about another appointment. He didn't argue and while he finished writing up my measurements, he joked and gossiped about some of the most prominent businessmen in town.

The Company would gladly employ you, Mr. Whalen, in the newly expanded corporate and economic research department. You would travel a lot and have a chance to visit many remote parts of the world. The Company has recently become involved in some explorations off Indonesia. Our extensive surveys have given the area quite good marks as far as oil deposits are concerned. The Far East, Mr. Whalen, may prove to contain oil deposits bigger than those of the Middle East. Our only problems are political. If the oil is there, and we think it is, we must successfully negotiate with those in power. Our country's relationship with Indonesia, for example, is extremely vital. Do you realize that the Asian oil market is the fastest-growing in the world? By the end of this decade, the Japanese will consume well over eleven million barrels a day. And keep in mind that Southeast Asia contains enough offshore crude oil to feed that growth.

Right now, though, its production capacity is minimal. Indonesia is presently the largest oil producer in Asia, but it turns out fewer than one million barrels a day. The Japanese have to rely on the Arabs for almost all their oil. They would prefer South Asian oil because it's close to their own market and the transportation costs would be lower. In addition, the oil off Indonesia is low-sulfur, an important consideration in pollution control. This Company has embarked on long-term research in Indonesia's offshore areas, and we must hope that a stable Indonesia will assure us access to the oil.

Since publicizing our aims could trigger various pressures, we have to handle all this very delicately.

The auditorium grew silent. The lights dimmed; only one bright spotlight followed the frail man who walked slowly towards the marble podium. The all-male audience sat motionless, its gaze fixed upon him. The man stumbled on one of the steep steps leading to the podium, but promptly recovered his balance. No one moved. Whalen was acutely aware that he had let himself get caught in an irreversible process. Only now did he understand what Susan once said to Karen: "Of all mammals, only a human being can say 'no.' A cow cannot imagine itself apart from the herd. That's why one cow is like any other. To say 'yes' is to follow the mass, to do what is commonly expected. To say 'no' is to deny the crowd, to be set apart, to reaffirm yourself."

The Secretary reached the lectern, caught his breath, and then in a trembling voice intoned:

"Every association of men with common objectives should set itself certain goals which its members hope to attain through the strength of their mutual sympathy and fellowship. We have declared the following to be the aims of this Order: to foster the high ideals of manly character and achievement, to improve our character through intellectual pursuits, and to unite ourselves in lasting friendship and loyalty.

"But in the enthusiasm of our striving we must not forget that the individual comes first along with his virtues: honorable ambition, fair speech, pure thoughts, and straightforward action.

"You, Jonathan James Whalen, are to be initiated into this Order, whose goals and purposes have just been declared. It is because the Brothers have thought you worthy of our trust that we have brought you into our fellowship. We invite you to share our privileges, we offer you our friendship and our loyal help in all your endeavors. We believe you are in sympathy with the goals of the Brotherhood and are prepared to make them your own. If we have erred and if you find in our goals that which is incompatible with your own highest ideals, it is your obligation here and now to declare it."

The spotlight left the stage and settled on Whalen. The entire audience turned towards him. He sat rigid and mute. The Secretary continued:

"Jonathan James Whalen, you will now rise, turn to face the Brothers and declare your solemn assent to our purposes."

The lights in the room brightened. Whalen rose and heard his voice reciting: "I promise and make covenant with the Brothers of this Order present and absent to obey the constitution, traditions and bylaws of this Order and to forward in every way within my power the objectives and aims for which it exists. So help me God."

I'm applying for the job, Mr. Whalen, because I'm tired. I live alone. My wife died, my children are grown and I don't even know where they are or with whom they live. For the last five years I've been delivering small planes from the manufacturers to buyers in Europe, Latin America, Africa and Japan. Did you know it's cheaper to deliver a small plane by flying it than by shipping it? The factory just removes everything unnecessary, fills the unused space with additional fuel tanks and reinforces the plane's landing gear to absorb this new weight, so you can fly twice the normal flying range if you have to, and you often do. And since "straight-from-the-assembly-line" planes usually have plenty wrong with them, you just have to keep flying and make as few overloaded landings and take-offs as possible. There are about fifty intercontinental ferry pilots in this country, and one out of ten gets killed every year. Maybe that's why one of them just called it quits.

This will be a very leisurely trip, Walter, and while we're together, there are a lot of things I would like to learn from you and Helen about my father and the Company.

I've chartered a jet plane, Gulfstream II, to take us to

Mombasa. This plane can normally carry as many as thirty passengers but I've had this one refurnished for the three of us. I've arranged for a villa at Ukunda, which is near Mombasa. It has an adjoining airstrip long enough to accommodate the Lockheed JetStar, our second plane, which has been modified to take off and land on a very short runway. We'll be able to fly into regions even the poachers can't reach.

At this time of year the climate is very mild on the Indian Ocean. I do hope you and Helen will accept. We could leave next week.

Breakfast was served on the terrace overlooking the ocean. Whalen handed Howmet the binoculars. "And that's a baobab tree," he said, pointing at the garden. "The native calls the baobab 'the devil tree' because he claims that the devil, getting tangled in its branches, punished the tree by reversing it. To the native, the roots are branches now, and the branches are roots. To ensure that there would be no more baobabs, the devil destroyed all the young ones. That's why, the native says, there are only full-grown baobab trees left."

Whalen turned towards the ocean. "Look at the reef," he said. "It's a natural barrier, protecting our shallows from sharks, and it stretches out for miles. The ocean is an enormous aquarium. You see anemones and coral and some of nature's most exotic creatures in the Indian Ocean."

"This is so thoughtful of you, Jonathan," said Howmet, gently tapping the shell of his egg with a knife. "Mrs. Howmet and I would never have come on our own, would we, Helen?"

Mrs. Howmet's voice was animated. "I just can't believe it! Only the day before yesterday we were in Woodbury, Connecticut. Look where we are now." She took the binoculars from her husband and scanned the shiny shallows directly before them.

After breakfast Whalen ordered the servants to prepare the rubber dinghy, his scuba equipment, sandwiches, drinks and fruits. He told them that he would be spending the day exploring the shallows with his guests and that they would all lunch on one of the sand bars near the reef.

He went to his room to check the tide table. Soon the rising tide would flow over the reef and start filling the shallows. From his balcony he saw the Howmets walking towards the beach. Whalen went down and helped Mrs. Howmet into the dinghy while a black servant steadied it. Whalen and Howmet pushed the boat in front of them, padding after it until they were up to their knees in water. When Howmet grew tired, Whalen helped him into the boat, then climbed in himself and started the small engine. The boat moved slowly through the clear water. The Howmets peered at the sea bed through the boat's transparent bottom, exclaiming whenever a big fish angled upward as if to attack. Whalen steered the boat diagonally towards the horizon, and in minutes they could no longer see Ukunda beach. Howmet turned on his movie camera and his wife waved at it, leaning out over the water against a background of grey-and-green jungle.

"My mother once told me," said Whalen, "that my father divided all people he had ever known into two groups—the wets and the drys. He only trusted people who perspired, because he believed that they couldn't lie without being betrayed by their sweat. He never trusted people who didn't perspire. I can see that even in this heat you don't perspire easily, Walter."

They were far from the mainland and could hear the surf crashing on the other side of the reef. Whalen selected the widest sand bar for landing. He pulled the boat onto the sand and helped his passengers disembark. He and Howmet removed the supplies from the boat, and Whalen stretched a beach blanket in the center of the sand bar. Meanwhile, Mrs. Howmet, who wore a large straw sun hat, filmed the colorful starfish spread near the water's edge.

"This is really paradise," Howmet exclaimed. "A little island in the middle of the ocean, miles away from the shore, from other beaches, from anything. How did you find such a place, Jonathan?"

"I came here once before," Whalen said, "to watch a sand-yacht race, nearby, on Bahati Beach. Later I learned how to sand-sail here." He collected his underwater gear while Mrs. Howmet kept filming.

"How long has this island been here?" asked Mrs. Howmet, pointing at the sand bar under her feet. "It's so clean. Only these few starfish. It looks as if it's just been washed." Whalen stared through the binoculars. There were no boats, no native dugouts, no one on the beach. The world was empty.

"I guess the ocean does wash over it once in a while, particularly if there's a storm," Whalen answered distractedly. He was listening to the sound of the surf swelling up behind the reef.

Mrs. Howmet filmed her husband as he helped Whalen

fasten his air tanks. When everything was ready, Whalen sat down on the edge of the bar and slid into the water. He dived towards the coral bed, and swam along the sand bar, frightening schools of fish which zigzagged around him. In one of the coral crannies he saw a blue blowfish. When the fish puffed up, he cornered and caught it, cradling it in his hands. He emerged at the sand bar, surprising the Howmets, who rested on the blanket with their ankles crossed, their pale wrinkled faces half hidden under their hats. The blowfish seemed about to explode, and while Mrs. Howmet filmed it, her husband took still photographs of her filming the fish and Whalen.

"I'll leave you both for a while now," said Whalen. "I think there are sea snakes around and I want to catch one."

"Be careful, Jonathan," said Howmet. "Remember Jonah!" He didn't seem to mind Whalen's leaving them alone. Mrs. Howmet waved her hand, smiling broadly. Then they both lay back, pulling their hats over their faces for a nap in the sun. As Whalen passed the dinghy he dropped the blowfish back into the sea and threw the boat's towrope overboard. Under water he grabbed the rope and eased the boat slowly off its perch. Once free of the sand bar the dinghy, pushed by the wind and incoming tide, floated away. Whalen began his long swim towards Ukunda. After a few minutes he surfaced and looked back. The Howmets had become two spots in the center of a small patch of yellow sand. The aimlessly drifting boat was barely visible, but the Howmets hadn't noticed it yet. Whalen submerged and continued to glide through the shallows cooled by the rush of water brought in by the tide and darkened by the sand stirred up and whirling in clouds.

When Whalen rose and looked back, the sand bar, like a water skier cut from a towrope, had vanished.

Whalen took off his mask. The jungle was still, the sky cloudless, the sea tranquil. The world was in order. Whalen swam towards Ukunda.

When he reached the villa he woke up the servants dozing on the terrace and instructed them to launch the two-engine motorboat. He explained that while he was skin-diving, his guests had gone exploring in the dinghy. Now, he said, he wanted them brought back for tea.

Whalen felt energy flowing into him from outside as if he were a starving man being nourished from an unknown source. Several times in broad daylight he was almost overcome by a need to sleep and then suddenly by a need to act. Deep within himself he could hear a child's laughter provoking urges that could not be satisfied by physical movement.

There were times when he lived on the far side of communicable thoughts and feelings. He fought these moments, trying to tear off the membrane that seemed to enclose his mind and inhibit his will. But he was helpless and possessed, beyond self-control.

The man entered and shook Whalen's hand. "How do you do, Mr. Whalen. I'm glad to know you." He took off his raincoat and waited for Whalen to sit down.

"I'm happy my lawyers were able to convince you to come here," said Whalen. "I hope you're not too inconvenienced by the suddenness of the trip."

"Not at all. I'm delighted. I've always wanted to spend more time in New York, but I was never able to." As he spoke, his accent became more apparent.

A waiter approached and served their drinks. Whalen raised his glass. The man responded and they both drank silently.

"I asked you to come here because I want your honest advice. I want to—" Whalen hesitated, sipping his drink—"I want to become an accomplished sportsman. In a very short time."

"So I understand. The lawyer who met me at the airport told me."

"He did not tell you that I'm no good at sports. The last time I skied, I was a boy. My father taught me swimming and golf. Apparently I couldn't concentrate or wasn't interested enough. At Yale I lost every competition I entered. I'm a terrible surfer. I don't like horse racing, fencing or handball." He paused. "You were the fastest skier in the Olympics. Tell me now, can you make me good enough to win the downhill in the World Alpine Competition?"

"Downhill?"

"Yes. You know how much I'm willing to pay for the training. What my lawyer didn't tell you is that if I win, I will pay you five times that amount."

"One question, Mr. Whalen. Why did you choose skiing? Why not gliding, car or boat racing, or tennis? There are many accomplished coaches who—"

"Because everybody would know that I could afford to have the latest, safest, and fastest glider, boat or car. And in tennis you have to play a whole series of matches."

"I see. And why the downhill?"

"It appeals to me. It's straight. No tricks."

"There's not much time left this season. You really want to try to win the competition?"

"I do. And I'm not a born winner. What do you say?"

The man got up and paced the room. "I don't want to discourage you, Mr. Whalen, but for such a crash-training program," he said, "we'll need the help of an orthopedist, and an expert in physical rehabilitation. You will have to build up your feet, legs and abdomen. We will start high-speed skiing in Les Diablerets and on other glaciers accessible by plane or helicopter. With this kind of rapid training you will have to wear devices to help protect you in bad falls. A battery-powered gyroscope, a model no larger than a bicycle's wheel, will have to be ordered right away. You'll carry it while skiing. It should help you learn the turns. Throughout your training we will employ four video cameramen, all good skiers themselves. They'll film you from different angles during every run. The advantage is that afterwards we can stop, reverse the tape on each of the videos and analyze your faults on their own small screens. By the end of the day we can examine the tapes on a large screen, where you can see yourself even better."

She undid the top button of her blouse and with a single movement crossed her arms and lifted the thin fabric over her head. He saw how white her skin was and how her breasts quivered as she shifted her body to unzip her skirt and slide it over her hips. Still looking at him she hooked her thumbs in the waistband of her black slip and pushed it very slowly down to her ankles. Then she undid her bra and stepped away from the pile of clothing.

She bowed her head, lay down and spread her hands on the rug. Her calves tensed as she thrust out her toes. Her skin felt dry and cool against him, but soon he could not distinguish between her flesh and his own. He stared at the mirror propped against the wall and saw himself slip into her. He probed deeper within her. Her face glistened in the light, her legs opened wide, her fingers laced behind his back.

In the mirror both of them looked swollen, doubled up, clutching each other, holding and thrusting. Still fixed on their reflection, Whalen withdrew, stood up and brushed his hair back from his forehead.

He picked her up and sat her on the arm of an overstuffed chair. He raised his hand and brought it down rapidly. Her resilient flesh whitened under the impact of his palm, then reddened immediately. He struck her again, harder this time, and heard her faint gasp.

205

She grasped the banister, and her lips parted as if she were going to cry out. Her hair fell over her face and he could no longer see her eyes. She remained motionless. He waited for her to do something. Then hoping to make her react, he walked to the opposite side of the staircase, opened the door to his room, entered and shut the door behind him.

During the week that followed, Whalen grew sick but the clinic's doctors wouldn't tell him what was wrong or prescribe any drugs. He had his bed rolled out onto the small terrace beyond his room and lay fully dressed, staring at the sky. He did not know why he was in pain. He only wanted his mind turned off. The life of the clinic and the town was of no interest to him. When the nurses chatted with him, he forced himself to smile and talk, but soon the effort exceeded his strength.

Even with the shutters of his room closed, and without opening his eyes, he could sense the coming of day. He rose before the staff and lay listening for the first familiar sounds: the rumbling of a bus through the streets, the buzz of a motorboat on the lake.

At night, when everything was quiet, he listened for occasional footsteps wandering through the clinic's empty corridors. The sounds were merely familiar; they did not affect him. In the early-morning sunshine, he lay like a stone on the shore, unmoved by the waves of spring air washing over him. A heavy weight constantly seemed to press against his chest. Voices became abstractions, separated from the bodies of people moving around him. He sensed only surfaces. Forms became empty figures without gravity or weight. He closed his eyes, blotting out the flat shapes that used to have dimension and meaning in his life, and the sounds that used to have resonance.

Once in a while he longed for some change and realized that this longing might be a prelude to recovery. But the very effort of hoping tired him; the weight settled down on his chest again and he lay back exhausted. All he wanted was to endure.

One night his body refused to sleep. He rose, left the clinic and walked directly to the shore of the lake. A sheet of mist rolled along the water, hiding all but the banks from view. The smell of moss spread through the air. He sniffed the dew, listened to the lapping of the water against the stones and felt the skin on the back of his neck prickle. The fog began to lift. He stared across the lake and saw the blinking lights of the villas and hotels of Geneva.

Jerzy Kosinski was born in Poland in 1933. He arrived in the United States in 1957 and completed his graduate and post-graduate education here.

Mr. Kosinski, who writes only in English, is the author of three previous novels: *The Painted Bird,* which won France's Best Foreign Book Award; *Steps,* which won the National Book Award for Fiction; and *Being There.* His nonfiction includes literary criticism and two volumes on collective behavior, *The Future Is Ours, Comrade* and *No Third Path,* both published under the pen name Joseph Novak. Mr. Kosinski's books have been translated into every major language.

Jerzy Kosinski has been both a Ford and a Guggenheim fellow, and a recipient of the Award for Literature of the National Institute of Arts and Letters. He has taught at Wesleyan and Princeton, and is presently Professor of Prose and Criticism at Yale University.